"I expected you t
nun's habit," Pas

"I chose not to become a *Because of you.*

But his eyes narrowed anyway. "I thought that was your life's ambition. Was it not?"

"People change."

"You seem markedly changed, in fact. One might even say distinctly hardened."

"I'm no longer a foolish girl easily taken advantage of by traveling soldiers, if that's what you mean."

His head canted to one side, and his black eyes gleamed. "Did I take advantage of you, Cecilia? That's not how I recall it."

She eyed him. "Whether you recall it that way or not, that's how it was."

"Tell me, then, how precisely did I take advantage of you? Was it when you crawled into my hospital bed, threw your leg over me and then rode us both to a mad finish?"

She remembered it as he said it. She remembered everything. The wonder of taking him inside her. The madness, the dizzy whirl. His big hands wrapped around her hips and his intent, ferociously greedy gaze.

No one had ever explained to her that the trouble with temptation was that it felt like coming home, wreathed in light and glory.

Secret Heirs of Billionaires

There are some things money can't buy...

Living life at lightning pace, these magnates are no strangers to stakes at their highest. It seems they've got it all... That is, until they find out that there's an unplanned item to add to their list of accomplishments!

Achieved:

1. Successful business empire.

2. Beautiful women in their bed.

3. *An heir to bear their name?*

Though every billionaire needs to leave his legacy in safe hands, discovering a secret heir shakes up the carefully orchestrated plan in more ways than one!

Uncover their secrets in:

Claimed for the Sheikh's Shock Son by Carol Marinelli

Shock Heir for the King by Clare Connelly

Demanding His Hidden Heir by Jackie Ashenden

The Maid's Spanish Secret by Dani Collins

Sheikh's Royal Baby Revelation by Annie West

Cinderella's Scandalous Secret by Melanie Milburne

Look out for more stories in the
Secret Heirs of Billionaires series coming soon!

Caitlin Crews

UNWRAPPING THE INNOCENT'S SECRET

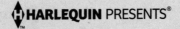

Recycling programs for this product may not exist in your area.

ISBN-13: 978-1-335-47877-1

Unwrapping the Innocent's Secret

First North American publication 2019

Printed in U.S.A.

USA TODAY bestselling and RITA® Award–nominated author **Caitlin Crews** loves writing romance. She teaches her favorite romance novels in creative-writing classes at places like UCLA Extension's prestigious Writers' Program, where she finally gets to utilize the MA and PhD in English literature she received from the University of York in England. She currently lives in the Pacific Northwest with her very own hero and too many pets. Visit her at caitlincrews.com.

Books by Caitlin Crews

Harlequin Presents

Conveniently Wed!

Imprisoned by the Greek's Ring
My Bought Virgin Wife

One Night With Consequences

A Baby to Bind His Bride

Bound to the Desert King

Sheikh's Secret Love-Child

Stolen Brides

The Bride's Baby of Shame

The Combe Family Scandals

The Italian's Twin Consequences
Untamed Billionaire's Innocent Bride
His Two Royal Secrets

Visit the Author Profile page
at Harlequin.com for more titles.

To all our wonderful Presents readers—this one is for you!

CHAPTER ONE

"I BEG YOUR PARDON, sir," his secretary said in the pointedly diffident way that always managed to convey the full range of his feelings.

Pascal Furlani shared them.

And he was not a man who ordinarilyf accepted the existence of feelings, unless they suited him. Or benefited him in some way.

"I have taken the liberty of compiling yet another slate of candidates," Guglielmo continued in that same tone, because he was not the sort of secretary who was afraid to share his opinions, feelings, or thoughts, however he might dress them up. "As the last several met with disfavor."

There was a dig in that, Pascal knew. He stood, not at the window that looked out over one of Rome's wealthiest neighborhoods, but at the glass partition that separated him from the rest of his sleek, modern office. It was the perfect antidote to the fussiness and great weight of Roman history everywhere else in the city.

Pascal knew too well what the three-thousand-year-old city looked like, from its forgotten streets to its most renowned *piazzas*. He knew how it felt to grow up rough and ignored in the shadow of the ruins of former great glories. And what life in this city had made him, the cast-off bastard son of a man who acknowledged only his legitimate issue and turned his back entirely on his mistakes.

He had earned every inch of the sweeping views his office commanded, but he was far prouder of what he'd done inside the walls of The Furlani Company.

Pascal had considered it a decent start when his personal wealth exceeded not only that of his father, but of all his father's legitimate children, too. Combined. He'd achieved that milestone in the first year after the accident.

The accident.

Pascal's lips thinned in inevitable displeasure as his mind tugged him back to the period of his life he most wanted to forget. The one stretch of his life where he'd lost focus. Where he'd come *this close* to forgetting himself completely.

He would never forget that his father had thrown him away like so much trash. He refused to forgive it. He did not hunger for revenge, necessarily—he wanted his life to be its own reckoning. Pascal chose to dominate from afar and show his father precisely as much interest as had been shown to him. And he had not wavered in this purpose since he'd been a small boy—save for that one regrettable winter.

It was not every man who could say that his rise from the ashes was not metaphoric, but entirely literal. The way they always did, Pascal's fingers found the grooves on his jaw that told the tale of the car crash that had left him scarred forever.

He quite liked them. The scars reminded him who he was and where he'd been, and how close he'd come to walking away from his purpose and ambition for what was, in the end, such a small temptation.

Not that his memories of that time were…small, exactly.

Nonetheless, the office reminded him where he was going. What he'd built with his own hands and force of will. It reinforced his goals. All of them sleek, moneyed, and each a pointed jab at the father who had never claimed him and the memory of a lost mother who had left him to his fate with no more than a shrug.

He had no intention of forgetting every last moment of how he'd come to be here.

"If you'll turn your attention to your tablet, sir," came his secretary's voice, excessively placid. Its own pointed jab, as usual. "I have arranged a selection of heiresses for your viewing pleasure, ordered in terms of their social standing."

Pascal turned away from his offices, all that granite and steel that he found so comforting here in the middle of ancient Rome. The building was filled to bursting with his vision. His money. His people acting to bring his dreams to fruition.

It was time for him to take the next step and find a wife.

Whether Pascal *wanted* to be married had little to do with it. A wife would make him look more stable, more settled, which some of the more conservative accounts preferred. A wife would conceivably keep him out of the tabloids, which his board would certainly prefer. And a wife would give Pascal legitimate heirs to his fortune and power.

Pascal would die before he consigned a child of his to the things he'd suffered, first and foremost being the lack of his father's name.

In addition, getting married would put an end to the mutterings of his board. That Pascal, as a single man with healthy appetites, was an embarrassment to his own company. That Pascal was somehow less trustworthy than other CEOs, imbued as they all were with wives and children, all legitimate and legal.

No one ever mentioned the mistresses and unclaimed bastards on the side, of course. No one ever did.

Pascal dropped his hand from his jaw. Something about his scars—which he knew were faded now to white instead of the angry red they'd been at first— was making him maudlin today.

Welcome to December, a voice inside him said. Snidely.

He knew what time of year it was. And why his thoughts kept returning to the crash and the flames that had very nearly been the end of him. But he had no intention of celebrating that anniversary. He never did.

He eyed his secretary, waiting with obvious impatience, instead.

"What makes you think that this collection of desperate, grasping socialites will be more appealing than the last?" he asked.

"Are we looking for *appealing*, sir? I'm not sure I had that on my list. I was looking more for *suitable*."

Pascal was sure he saw the hint of a smirk on his secretary's face, though the other man knew better than to succumb in full.

"Careful, Guglielmo," he murmured. "Or I may begin to suspect that you do not take this enterprise as seriously as you should."

He walked back to his desk, a massive slab of granite that looked like what it was. A throne and a monument to Pascal's hard-won power and influence. Guglielmo gestured toward the tablet computer that lay in the center, and Pascal checked a sigh as he picked it up and scrolled through the offerings.

Lady this, daughter of Somebody Pedigreed, the toast of this or that finishing school. The daughter of a Chinese philanthropist. Two French girls from separate families that were connected—somewhere back in the deep, dark, tangled roots of their family trees—to ancient kings and queens. An Argentinian heiress, raised on cattle money halfway across the world.

They were all beautiful, in their way. If not classically so, then polished to shine. They were all accomplished, in one way or another. One ran her own charity. One performed the flute with a world-renowned orchestra. Another spent the bulk of her time on humanitarian missions. And not one of them had ever been mentioned in a tabloid newspaper.

Pascal refused to consider anyone with a whiff of paparazzi interest about them or near them, like the California wine heiress who was herself marvelously spotless, but had been best friends since boarding school with a celebrity whose life played out in headlines across the globe. No, thank you. He wanted no scandals. No dark secrets, poised to emerge at the worst possible time. No secrets at all, come to that.

Pascal was a scandal. His whole life had been first a secret, then a shock, trumpeted in headlines of its own. His tawdry, illegitimate birth and his shipping magnate father's steadfast refusal to acknowledge his existence throughout his life might as well have been another set of scars on the other side of his face. He had always felt marked by the circumstances of his birth, his parents' poor choices.

He would always be marked by these things.

His wife, accordingly, had to be without stain.

"You do not look pleased, sir," Guglielmo said drily. "Yet again. I fear I must remind you that an unblemished heiress of reasonable social standing is, in fact, a finite resource. One we may have exhausted." He inclined his head slightly when Pascal glared at him. "Sir."

"I'm meeting with the last of the previous selection of possibilities tonight," Pascal reminded him.

"I made the reservation myself, sir. Moments after you informed me that the meeting you'd had with another woman on that list was, in your words, appalling beyond reason."

"She did not resemble her photograph," Pascal said darkly.

"Sadly, that is part and parcel of the digital dating culture we all now—"

"Guglielmo. She was a sweet-looking, conservatively dressed blonde in the pictures you showed me. She showed up with a blue and pink Mohawk and a sleeve of tattoos. I liked her more that way, if I am honest, but I can hardly parade a punk rock princess in front of my board. If I could, I would."

"The woman you're meeting tonight has a robust social media presence and absolutely no hint of punk rock about her," Guglielmo replied blandly. "I checked myself."

Pascal found his fingers on his scars again. "Perhaps I will be swept away tonight and all of this will prove unnecessary."

"Hope springs eternal," Guglielmo murmured.

After Pascal dismissed him, he didn't launch himself into one of the numerous tasks awaiting his attention. He could see his emails piling up. His message light was blinking. But instead of handling them he found himself sitting at his desk, scowling out at the physical evidence of the empire he'd built. Brick by bloody brick.

Because once again, the only thing in his head was her.

His angel of mercy. His greatest temptation.

The woman who had nearly wrecked him before he'd begun.

It is December, he reminded himself. *This is always how it feels in December. Come the New Year she will fade again, the way she always does.*

His phone rang, snapping him back to reality and far away from that godforsaken northern village in a forgotten valley in the Dolomites. Where he had crashed and burned—literally.

And she had nursed him back to life.

Then had haunted him ever since, for his sins.

Tonight, he vowed as he turned his attention to the tasks awaiting him, he would leave the past where it belonged, and concentrate on the next bright part of his glorious future.

"I think it's important to set very clear boundaries from the start," his date informed him much later that evening. She had arrived late, clearly full of herself in her role as a minor member of the Danish nobility. She had swept into one of the most exclusive restaurants in Rome with her nose in the air, as if Pascal had suggested she meet him at one of those sticky, plastic American fast food restaurants. Her expression had not improved over the course of their initial drinks. "Obviously, the point of any merger is to secure the line."

"The line?"

"I am prepared to commit to an heir and a spare," she told him loftily. "To be commenced and completed within a four-year period. And I think it's best to agree, up front and in writing, that the production of any progeny should be conducted under controlled circumstances."

Pascal was sure he'd had more romantic conversations on industrial sites.

"Is it a production line?" he asked, his voice dry. "A factory of some kind?"

"I already have an excellent fertility specialist, discreet and capable, who can ensure to everyone's satisfaction and all legalities that the correct DNA carries on into the next generation."

Pascal blinked at that. He had had simpering dinners. Overtly sexual ones. Direct, frank approaches. But this was new. It all seemed so…mechanical.

"You are staring at me as if I've said something astonishing," his date said.

"I beg your pardon." Pascal attempted to smile, though he wasn't sure when or if he'd ever felt less charming. "Are you suggesting that we concoct offspring in a laboratory? Rather than go about making them in the more time-honored fashion, favored as it has been for a great many eons already?"

"This is a business arrangement," his chilly date replied, looking, if possible, more severe than before. "I expect you will find your release elsewhere, as will I. Discreetly, of course. I do not hold with scandal."

"Nothing is less scandalous than a sexless marriage, naturally."

A faint suggestion of a line appeared between her perfectly shaped brows. "There's no need to muddy a perfectly functional marriage with that sort of thing, surely."

"You've thought of everything," he replied.

And later, after he had left his date with a curt nod and an insincere promise to have his people contact her, Pascal waved off his driver and walked instead.

Because Rome was its own reward. The city of his birth and his poverty-stricken childhood. The city where he had become a man, by his own estimation, then joined the military to give himself what his mother couldn't and his father would never. Discipline. A life. Even a career. It had seemed such an elegant solution.

Until that night six years ago when he'd followed a reckless whim, on a moody December night very much like this one. It had been raining in Rome. He'd hoped that meant it was snowing in the Dolomites, on the edge of the Alps, and had decided he might as well drive himself up north and learn how to ski.

He laughed a bit at that as he moved through Piazza Navona and its annual Christmas Market that made the crowded square even more filled and frenetic. He dodged the usual stream of tourists and his own countrymen, taking in the night air and already surrendering to the pollution of Christmas that would invade everything until the Epiphany, then thankfully disappear into the clarity of the New Year.

The night was cold and leaning toward dampness. It was the perfect sort of weather to ask himself how he'd ended up with the coldest, most clinical woman imaginable tonight. Was that really what he was reduced to? A laboratory experiment masquerading as a marriage?

He knew he needed to marry, but somehow, he had imagined it would be…less cold-blooded. Warmer. Or cordial, at the very least.

And he wanted to make his babies his own damned self. More than that, he had no intention of following in his father's footsteps in any regard. Once he married, Pascal had no intention of cheating. He was not planning to have "arrangements" on the side. He wasn't planning on having an *on the side*, for that matter.

He had no intention of creating another woman like his mother, so fragile and so lost she couldn't take care of her own son. And he would never, ever risk the possibility that he might create an illegitimate child of his own.

The very idea made him sick.

His phone buzzed in his pocket, and he knew it was Guglielmo, checking in the way he always did after these excruciating "dates" that were little more than vetting sessions. Because Pascal persisted in imagining that he could cut through all the nonsense, ask for exactly what he wanted and then get it. It had worked in business, why not in marriage?

Pascal didn't answer the call.

There were a million more things that required his attention, but he couldn't face them just yet. Instead, he lost himself in the chaotic embrace of the Eternal City. Rome was a monument, yet Rome was ever-changing. Rome was a contradiction. Rome was where Pascal felt alive. It was the place where he had grown to understand that his very existence was an affront to some, and it was where he finally figured out how to claim that existence and make sense of it.

Walking through Rome had always soothed him. And kept him alive, some dark years. Long nights with his feet, his thoughts and the grand Roman sprawl had made him whole, time and time again.

So there was no reason at all that he should be caught up in memories of a tiny, sleepy village with steep mountains all around and very few people, where he had never been anything but broken.

He stopped by a fountain in a forgotten courtyard, steps from the roar of a busy road. The water tumbled from the pursed lips of an old god made stone, and in the dark, he almost believed he could see her reflection there in the water the way he always did in his head.

Sweet Cecilia, half nurse and half angel. A woman so lovely and so innocent that he had nearly betrayed every vow he'd ever made to himself and stayed up there in all that towering silence.

The very notion was absurd. He was Pascal Furlani. Not for him the pastoral delights, such as they were, of a remote mountain village of interest to absolutely no one unless they happened to either have been there for centuries or were a part of the quiet abbey that had also been there, in one form or another, since right about the dawn of time. Not for him a life forgotten and tucked away like that, out of sight.

She would have taken her vows by now, Pascal assumed, and become a full nun like the others in the order. Or perhaps his last, half-dreamt night there had been her fall from grace. Would she have stayed?

Taken her place outside the abbey walls? Perhaps she lived in the village proper now, or off in the fields that dotted the hillsides with some or other farmer. She would be settled now, one way or the other. Committed to her Lord or married to some man, and unrecognizable.

Just as he was.

Pascal was not haunted by the specter of his childhood. He had lived through it, transcended it and moved on. He had mourned his mother's death, then buried her with greater reverence than she had ever shown him. He rarely thought of his father these days, preferring to decimate the old man and his penny-tante shipping concern from afar.

Pascal did not look back. Ever.

Unless it was to her. Cecilia.

His personal ghost.

"Enough," he muttered. He pulled a coin from his pocket, then flipped it to the air, watching as it tumbled into the water before him. He had made his last reckless decision the night he'd chosen to drive like a maniac up into those mountains in search of one of Italy's many ski resorts. He had been on leave from the army and the idea—or some demon—had seized him, which in those days was all Pascal needed. That and a bottle of something strong.

He had never made it to a ski resort. He'd spun out on a mountain pass after making a wrong turn. The clunker of a car he'd been driving—good for absolutely nothing save ejecting him through the windshield with great force—was the only reason he'd lived.

The car had burst into flames, and Pascal would have burned, too, had he not been tossed off into the unforgiving wilderness.

But even the fire was a blessing in disguise. It had alerted the villagers. They'd trooped out in the middle of the dark December night, collected his broken body and had settled him into what passed for the local hospital. The clinic connected to the abbey, where slowly, carefully, the nuns had nursed him back to health.

Pascal had been torn open, broken and out of his mind for weeks. It had taken him longer than that to heal. Then painfully learn how to move again when the casts came off.

And the greatest danger of it all was not the infections he risked or the bones that healed differently than they'd been. It was not his discharge from the military, or the entirely new life he was forced to face—and figure out while lying flat on his back— thanks to the wreckage of the old.

It was the fact that life in that forgotten village felt sweet. Easy. *Good*.

It had been the greatest temptation of his life to simply…remain.

And his favorite nun had been a part of that.

Not quite a nun, he corrected himself now, his

hands deep in his pockets as he brooded at the fountain before him. She had been a novice of the order, young and sweet and uncorrupted—until she'd met him.

But when he thought of what happened between them, her cool smiles and soft hands, blooming into that one night of almost unbearable passion that still made his body stir after all these years—he couldn't help but think that she had been the one to do the corrupting.

He was a master of the universe by any reckoning, and yet...here he stood. In a dark, forgotten corner of the greatest city on earth, the world literally at his feet, her face in his memories making the city dim.

It was an outrage. It was unacceptable.

Pascal headed toward his home, three stories of the top of a building that he had refurbished to suit his particular taste. Distinctively modern inside and an appropriately battered, ancient-looking façade.

It was not lost on him that for all intents and purposes, that description could have been about him.

When he reached his building, he didn't go inside. He headed to his garage instead and somehow or another, almost without conscious thought, he found himself in one of his cars. Then heading north. This time he was neither as drunk nor as reckless as he'd been six years ago, but still. A man did not possess a car as fast as his if he did not plan to use it.

He drove for six hours, through what remained of

the night and into the dawn. He stopped for breakfast and strong coffee when he reached Verona. When the espresso had revived him sufficiently, he called Guglielmo to tell him where he was.

"And may I ask, sir, why you are a great many kilometers away from the office? May I assume that your meeting last night did not go as well as you hoped?"

"You may assume what you like," Pascal replied.

And as he lingered over another espresso, Pascal had ample time to ask himself what exactly he thought he was doing. The answer came to him after he'd gotten back on the road.

The months he'd spent in the care of that abbey was the only time in his life that he could recall straying so far from who he was, and he'd resented it ever since. Bitterly. Cecilia had been a kind of enchantment. A witch in a nun's habit.

He'd told himself he was well rid of her when he'd come back down the mountain and remembered himself at last. He'd meant it. He'd gone about creating his company and doing every last thing he'd ever dreamed.

And yet…he couldn't seem to move on. No matter how many empires he built, no matter how much richer he made himself, he was still haunted by her face.

It was high time for an exorcism.

Two hours later he found himself on the same

mountain where he'd nearly died six years ago. It was a cold, crisp morning in another December, and he treated the winding mountain road with a great deal more respect than he had back then.

And this time he pulled off to the side of the road when he reached the top, because he could see the village before him.

It looked like a storybook, which only made him more determined to scrape it off whatever passed for his battered soul. It was like a dream in the morning light. Snowcapped mountains all around, and down in the small valley, fields cut by a tumbling river. What passed for the center of town was a clump of old buildings that dated from centuries past. The church stood at one end of the village with the abbey behind it and off to one side, the hospital where he had survived his recovery. He stared at it a long while, aware that his fingers were on his scars again.

Something in him turned over, with a low hum.

He told himself it was sheer horror that a man like him, raised in the middle of one of the most frenetic and sophisticated cities in the world, not to mention the luxurious lifestyle he now enjoyed, should ever have imagined that he could stay here.

Here.

It beggared belief.

He started up the car again, following the road down and around and around, until it reached the valley floor.

Where everything was exactly as he'd left it.

There was no reason that his heart should be clattering about in his chest as he drove the familiar road to the church. He would find the old priest and ask after Cecilia. He would almost surely find such a reunion faintly horrifying, and once he did, he would leave. The truth was, he'd come a very great distance for what he expected to take all of a few moments. He could have—and should have—sent Guglielmo. Or some other underling, who could have reported back on whether Cecilia was still here. For that matter, there had been no earthly reason for him to drive through the night like a man possessed. He could have taken his helicopter and landed it in the field behind the church, the same field he'd stared at week after week after week from his hospital bed.

No wonder he'd become fixated on the novice nun who'd cared for him. There had been nothing else to do. Except, Mother Superior had told him serenely, pray.

Pascal had not prayed then. He considered a prayer for deliverance now instead. Because he had surrendered to this fantasy for absolutely no good reason. This appalling tour through his own nostalgia.

"You might as well get it over with," he growled at himself.

He unfolded himself from the low-slung sports car and stood beside it a moment. It was midmorning now, and though it was a clear day, the wind rushed down from the mountain peaks and sliced straight through him. He was dressed for a sophisticated dinner in Rome, not a trip to the hinterland.

He adjusted the jacket of his bespoke suit with two impatient tugs of his hands, and didn't bother looking around. The village felt deserted. If memory served, what few villagers there were rarely congregated before the afternoon, if then. The nuns had chosen this valley well. It was the perfect spot for silent contemplation.

Pascal walked up the steps to the front door of the church. The weathered door stood open a crack, and he pushed his way inside, and then paused for a moment in the vestibule as he was walloped with memories.

It smelled the same. It looked the same. And it made his head spin as if he'd overindulged again.

What year is this? he asked himself.

The church might not have changed in the past century. But Pascal had changed tremendously since he'd left here. That was what he needed to remember.

He moved into the church proper, his gaze moving from the quiet, empty pews to the candles flickering in the alcoves. He saw no hint of the old, garrulous priest who he recalled so vividly from six years ago. The place was deserted—

But then he heard a noise. He took a few more steps and saw a washer woman on her hands and knees, scrubbing at the floor before the altar with her back to him.

She did not look around as he started down the aisle, and that gave Pascal ample opportunity to remember all the other times he'd done this exact same walk. All the times the priest had encouraged him to look within for a change, rather than continuing to look outside himself.

What is the point of all this power you seek if your heart is empty? the old man had asked him.

What do you know of either power or a heart? Pascal had replied. And he'd laughed.

But Pascal did not think the old man had been kidding. And those sneaky words were one more ghost that he couldn't quite get to leave him alone.

He dropped his gaze from the stained glass in the small nave, and stood there, several feet away from the woman on the floor. He expected her to stop what she was doing, for she must have heard him, but she didn't. Not even when he cleared his throat.

"If I might have a moment of your attention, *signorina*," he said, his voice echoing back at him from all around.

She moved then. She sat back on her knees, and tugged the headphones out of her ears in one smooth motion. And Pascal was caught, somehow, in the smoothness of it.

But then she shifted around to face him, still down there on the stone floor. And everything…stopped.

That face.

Her face.

He'd been seeing it for years.

He knew every millimeter of her heart-shaped face, and the rich brown hair touched with gold that surrounded it. He knew that wide, generous mouth, and the delicate nose.

Most of all, he knew those eyes. Startling violet set above cheekbones made for poetry.

He knew her, his angel of mercy and the ghost that had haunted him for years.

It was Cecilia. His Cecilia.

"My God," he whispered. "It's you."

"It's me," she replied, her voice flat. Hard. And that was when he noticed that those violet eyes of hers were bright on his. And murderous. "And you can't have him."

CHAPTER TWO

CECILIA REGINALD WAS no stranger to fear or disappointment.

It was right there in the name she'd been left with all those years ago when the English lady—her mother, presumably—had stayed in the only *pensione* in the village for the weekend, given a fake name, and then had left her three-year-old behind when she'd run off. Never to return.

Cecilia had always known that she was disposable, though she happily remembered very little of that first, lost life. Just as she'd always known that Pascal Furlani, who had discarded her when she was fully grown and able to recall every painful second of it, would be back.

At first, she had dreamed of his return. Wished for it, fervently, as if he'd disappeared from the village by mistake somehow. Because assuming he did the right thing—and she'd assumed he would then—would have solved her problems in a neat, orderly and time-honored fashion. Because his coming back would have made sense of the wreckage that her neat, orderly life had become in the chaotic wake he'd left behind him.

And because she had imagined herself *in love* with him.

But of course, that was not when he had deigned to tear himself away from his meteoric rise to wealth and prominence and return at long last. Not when she would have greeted his return with nothing short of delight. Instead, he came back now, when she wanted it least. And not only because she no longer believed in such childish notions as *being in love*.

"Who is *him*?" he asked. "And why do you imagine I would wish to *have him*, whatever that means?"

She didn't miss the affront in that deep, rich voice of his she'd done her best to forget. Or try to forget.

Just as she didn't miss the crack of power in it, either. It seared through her like a lightning strike and she added the unpleasant intensity of the sensation to the list of things she blamed him for.

Cecilia knelt there on the floor, her weight back on her heels, and her hands wet from scrubbing the stones. She had to crane her neck back to look up at him. Up and up and up, for he seemed much taller than she remembered him. While she imagined she looked shriveled and ruined and infinitely hardened by the years—because that was how she felt, certainly.

Back then she'd had faith. She'd believed that people were mostly good and life was certain to work out well, one way or another, even for abandoned girls like her.

She'd learned. Oh, how she'd learned.

Cecilia was fairly certain she wore every last lesson right there on her face.

Meanwhile Pascal looked like he'd stepped straight out of the pages of one of those glossy magazines she pretended she didn't know existed and had certainly never scoured, just to see his face. He looked like the lofty, arrogant man he'd gone off to become, leaving her here to handle the mess he'd made. And the man in those magazines bore no resemblance whatsoever to the broken, half-wild creature she'd taken far too much pleasure in nursing back to health.

If there had ever been anything broken in Pascal Furlani, she couldn't see it now. Were it not for the scars on the left side of his jaw that she knew continued down across his chest—though in her memory, they were far more raw and angry than the silver lines she could see today—she would have been hard-pressed to imagine that anything could ever have touched this man at all.

Much less her.

A thought that made her want to throw her bucket of dirty water at him. Preferably so it could damage that overtly resplendent suit he wore with entirely too much unconscious, masculine ease.

God, how she hated him.

The trouble was, it had been easy to scoff at those pictures of him. To tell herself that she was better off without a man who would go to such places, with such people, and dress the way he did when he was photographed. So breathlessly, deliberately fancy, which even she knew cost the kind of money she would never, ever have. Or even be near. The kind of money that was so dizzying she wouldn't *want* to have it. It was corrosive. Cecilia didn't have to live the high life in Rome to understand that.

Her life here had always been simple. Things were more complicated than she'd planned six years ago, but still. Overall, life was *simple.*

And nothing about Pascal Furlani was simple.

Neither was her reaction to him.

Cecilia had forgotten the way he filled a room. That antiseptic chamber in the clinic. This whole church. Just by standing there in all his state, his black eyes glittering.

The problem was he was so…arresting.

He had changed since he'd left the hospital, where he'd been so rangy and wiry. He'd filled in. He looked solid. *Big.* Strong, everywhere, with the kind of smooth, powerful muscles that quietly boasted of the worship he paid to his own body and the kind of power he could wield.

But Cecilia did not want to think too much about his body.

His dark hair was as she remembered it, cropped close to his head. It only made those glittering black-gold eyes of his all the more mesmerizing. Electric, even, like another lightning strike she had no choice but to endure while it lit her on fire.

He looked like a Roman centurion. His aquiline nose. His sensual lips. Something impassive and stern in the stark lines of him.

And she hated the fact that she knew how he tasted.

"You're not welcome here," she told him as evenly as she could from where she knelt there before him. "I already made that clear to your little spies. You didn't have to come all the way up into the mountains yourself."

He blinked, and made a small pageant out of it.

"I do not have spies, Cecilia."

Her name in that familiar, charged voice of his rolled through her, igniting fires she would have sworn only moments before had been doused forever.

"You can call them whatever you like." She had the urge to get to her feet, but ignored it, because scrambling up from her knees made it far more obvious that she was discomfited by their power differential. And she did not wish to be discomfited by Pascal Furlani. Not any more than she already had been. So she stayed put, meeting his gaze with defiance as if he was the one on the ground. "They said they were on the board of your company. You will forgive me if

I assumed that meant they had something to do with you. Or do you really expect me to believe that two visits from you and your minions over the course of three weeks is a random coincidence?"

He didn't appear to move and yet it was like a storm gathered around him. Cecilia was sure that if she looked down, she would see the fine hairs on her arms stand on end.

"Members of my board were here?" His voice was…darker. Midnight thunder.

It took her a moment to process the way he'd said *here*. As if this village where he'd nearly died and had come back to life again was so far beneath him that the very idea that anyone he knew from his fancy boardrooms might visit it appalled him.

Cecilia tried not to grit her teeth. "I will tell you what I told them. You have nothing to do with this place. Or with me. You left. And you don't get to swan back in here now, no matter the reason. I won't allow it."

His dark eyes flashed. "Will you not?"

Something about that question, too silky by half and far more dangerous than it should have been, had Cecilia tossing her sponge into her bucket. With perhaps too much force, she reflected, when water sloshed over the sides.

"What do you want, Pascal?" she demanded.

Through her gritted teeth.

He looked down at her from his irritatingly

great height. "I thought I came here to expel old ghosts."

"I don't believe you'd know a ghost if one appeared at the foot of your bed, wreathed in chains and moaning your name."

Again he blinked as if he expected the movement of his eyelids to bring underlings running to serve him. Something that likely occurred with depressing regularity down in Rome.

"You do not believe that you have haunted me these past years, *cara*?" And she couldn't say she cared for the way he used the endearment, either. Like a sharp-edged blade, and he wasn't afraid to cut her. "I cannot say I believe it, either. And yet here I am, when I vowed I would never return."

"I suggest you turn around, return to wherever you came from and uphold your vow."

He did not take her suggestion. Instead, he stayed where he was and studied her for a moment.

"I do not understand why my board would be at all interested in you," he said after what felt like an eternity. Or three. "I've never kept this part of my life a secret. Everyone knows I nearly died in the mountains and it changed me profoundly. I discuss it often enough. Why would they come here now? What could they hope to find here besides an old lover?"

Cecilia could hardly breathe. She couldn't imagine what expression she wore on her face. *An old lover.* Was that what she was to him? Was that all she was?

But she kept her cool, no matter what it cost her, because she had to. *She had to.* She would not react to the tightness in her chest. The shortness in her breath.

Or that wild, betraying tumult in her pulse.

All that she could chalk up to fear, she told herself as Pascal gazed down at her, arrogant and impatient. It was nothing but panic, surely. The strange feeling, too much like some kind of anticipation, she felt that her worst fear was being realized in the extraordinary flesh whether she liked it or not.

She could understand that. It was her other reactions that concerned her more. Most especially that melting low in her belly that told her terrible truths about her true feelings about Pascal's return that she wanted desperately to deny.

She got to her feet then, taking her time. And as she did, she was fiercely glad that she looked like who and what she was: a woman who washed floors for a living. She was nothing like the sorts of pampered women Pascal always had on his arm in the magazine pictures that were burned into her head. Cecilia knew she bore no resemblance to them and never would. She was not elegant. Her jeans were too big, decidedly ripped and horribly stained. She wore a ratty T-shirt beneath the long-sleeve buttoned-up shirt she'd tied off at her waist. Her hair was a disaster, no matter that she'd tied it back with an old scarf.

She expected she looked more or less tragic to a man like him. He was no doubt asking himself how he'd ever lowered himself to touch one such as her. She wondered it herself.

But this was a good thing, she told herself sternly. Because he needed to go away and never come back. And if she disgusted him now, well, she was only what she'd had to become. To survive him. If that got him to leave, great. Whatever worked.

She ignored the small pang that notion gave her.

"I expected you to be wearing a nun's habit," he said, and she opted not to hear the wicked undertone in his voice. Much less…remember the way she'd thrilled to it, once.

"I chose not to become a nun." She did not say, *because of you*.

But his eyes narrowed anyway. "I thought that was your life's ambition. Was it not?"

"People change."

"You seem markedly changed, in fact. One might even say, distinctly hardened."

"I'm no longer a foolish girl easily taken advantage of by traveling soldiers, if that's what you mean."

His head canted to one side, and his black eyes gleamed. "Did I take advantage of you, Cecilia? That's not how I recall it."

She eyed him. "Whether you recall it that way or not, that's how it was."

"Tell me, then, how precisely did I take advantage of you? Was it when you crawled into my hospital bed, threw your leg over me and then rode us both to a mad finish?"

She remembered it as he said it. She remembered everything. The wonder of taking him inside her. The madness, the dizzy whirl. His big hands wrapped around her hips and his intent, ferociously greedy gaze.

No one had ever explained to her that the trouble with temptation was that it felt like coming home, wreathed in light and glory.

That melting sensation grew worse, but she refused to let herself squirm the way she wanted to do.

Because this wasn't about her.

"I always wondered what it would be like to have a conversation like this with you," Cecilia said when she was sure she could manage to sound calm. Faintly bored. And it was not untrue, though as the years passed, the content of the conversation had changed in her head. She'd asked fewer questions. At some point she'd even become magnanimous. She'd practiced it enough in mirrors. "I find it's less productive than I might have imagined. I don't understand why you're here. *I* am not haunted."

Only furious, still and always, but she didn't tell him that. He didn't deserve to know.

"Can it be as simple as catching up with an old friend?" he asked as if he was…reasonable in any way. Palatable.

She made a scoffing sound. "Please. We were never friends."

To her surprise, his mouth curved. "Cecilia. Of course we were."

Something in her chest seemed to stutter to a halt then. Something different from the panic, the heat.

Because she remembered other things, too. Long afternoons when she would sit by his bedside, holding his hand or mopping his brow with a cool cloth. In those early days, when no one had known if he would make it, she'd sung to him. Songs of praise and joy interspersed with silly nursery rhymes and the like, all calculated to soothe.

When he grew stronger, he would tell her stories. He couldn't believe that she had never been to Rome. That she had never been more than a couple of hours out of this valley, for that matter. Or not that she could recall. He painted pictures for her with his words, of ancient ruins interspersed with traffic charging this way and that, sidewalk cafés, beautiful fountains. Later, when she was no longer a novitiate and often found herself up in the middle of the night—either because she was worried about her future, or because sleep was a rarity for a woman in her position—she'd looked up pictures online and found the city he described. In bright detail.

He'd made her feel as if she knew it personally. Sometimes she thought she hated him for that.

"Either way," she said resolutely, "we're not friends now. Do you wish to know how I know we're not? Because friends do not disappear like smoke in the middle of the night, without a word."

She regretted that the moment she said it. This was not about her, not anymore, and if she wanted to tell herself a harsh truth or two, it was possible it never had been. She could have been the field outside his window. The mountains looming about in every direction. She was simply *here*. He was the one who crashed the car, tore himself to pieces and got the luxury of telling dramatic stories about what the experience had taught him in televised interviews.

Not that she planned to admit she'd ever watched them.

Meanwhile, Cecilia was the one who could remember nothing but this valley. This village. The comfort of the abbey walls and the counsel of the women she'd believed would be her sisters one day.

It was true that he had taken all of that away from her. But another truth was that she'd given it to him. And she knew she shouldn't have mentioned that night.

Something she was in no doubt about when his expression changed. His eyes were too hot suddenly. His mouth was too stern and yet remained entirely too sensual.

Now that she was standing up, she could better appreciate what the years had done for his form. He had always been beautiful, like something carved from soft stone and twisted into that flesh that had healed so slowly. Now he seemed made of granite. His shoulders were so wide. And the excellent tailoring of the suit he wore did absolutely nothing to disguise the fact that his torso was thick with hard, solid muscle.

And somehow she'd expected that because he'd filled out he would be less tall. But he wasn't. She still had to look up at him. And for some reason, even though she was no longer on her knees, it made her feel a little too close to powerless for comfort.

"By all means," he said in that dark, silken way of his. "Let us discuss that night."

And she'd already started down this road. She might as well say all the things she'd been carrying around inside her all these years, or at least the highlights, because she had no intention of having this discussion again.

"What is there to discuss?" she asked. "I fell asleep in your arms. It was the first time I had done something like that, as every other moment we'd had together had been so furtive. Stolen. But not that night. You asked me to stay and I stayed. And when I woke up in the morning, you had left the valley for good." She made a noise that no one could mistake for a laugh. "In case you're wondering, I woke up the way you left me. Naked. With the sun beaming in the windows and Mother Superior standing at the foot of the bed."

Back then she could have read every expression that moved over his face. Every glint in his eye. But though she could see something shift there today, she couldn't twist it into any kind of sense. And it was stunning, the things that could wallop a person. The ways that grief could sneak into the most surprising crevices and well up there, like tears.

"Is that why you're not a nun?" he asked.

She wondered if he knew what a loaded question that was.

It is not for me to tell you what to do, child, Mother Superior had said when Cecilia's condition became clear. *That is between you and God. But I will tell you this. I have known you since you were delivered to our door. I watched you grow up. And I greeted, with joy, the notion that you might join the sisters here. But the truth is, the order is the only family you've known. I have to ask myself if you truly wish to dedicate yourself to this life, or if what you want most of all is family. And now you will have your own. Do you truly wish to give that up?*

"In the end," Cecilia said now to the man who was a catalyst for both her greatest shame and deepest joy in life, damn him, "I was not a good fit for the order."

"Not a good fit? You'd already been living in that abbey for most of your life. How could you not be perfect for them? Why would they let you walk away?"

She glared at him. "These are all interesting questions. But not from someone who ran off in the middle of the night. If you had questions to ask me, Pascal, you could have asked them then."

"I did not *run off*," he bit out. And if she wasn't mistaken, there was something like temper in his voice then. Sparking in that black gaze of his. "You must always have known, *cara*, that my destiny was never here."

Her palms stung and she realized she'd curled her hands into fists. She forced herself to unclench her fingers, one by one.

"That became clear once you left. And then failed to return for six years."

"I'm here now."

"And I'm sure that any moment, the heavens will open up and hosannas will rain down upon us all," Cecilia retorted. Archly. "But until that moment, you will forgive me if I am somewhat less enthused."

"The Cecilia I remember would never have spoken to me this way." One of his brows rose. Imperiously. "I remember soft, cool hands. A pretty singing voice. And cheeks that were forever pinkening."

"That girl was an idiot." Cecilia sniffed. "And she died six years ago, when she woke to find herself not at all the person she'd imagined herself to be."

"I don't know what that means."

"Don't you? I thought that I was a moral, upstanding, pure and wholesome individual. A woman who truly wished to dedicate herself to a life of service. But it turned out that I was wicked straight through, shameless enough to flaunt it in the very abbey that raised me, and so foolish that I actually believed that the man who had engineered my fall might stick around to help with a rough landing. Alas. He did not."

His stern mouth looked starker somehow. "I was told that all sins would be forgiven if I were to do what was inevitable, what I would do anyway, and leave."

Cecilia opened her mouth to argue that, but something about the way he said it tugged at her. "What do you mean, you were told?"

But he didn't answer the question. He studied her for a moment, then another, his hand on his jaw.

"You have yet to explain to me what my board members were doing here. Let me guess who it was. An older gentleman, perhaps? Silver hair and beard, a theatrical cane and a penchant for dressing like an uptight Victorian? And his trusty sidekick, the younger man, round and possessed of an overly glossy mustache?"

He had described the two men exactly.

She shrugged. "They didn't leave their names."

"But I can see from your expression that they were the ones who came here. Why?"

"Your story of narrowly escaping death in the Dolomites, and the recovery that allowed you ample time to shore up your scheme to take over the world, is practically a fairy tale told to small children at this point. Everyone has heard it."

"I'm delighted that you have paid such close attention."

"But that's my point," Cecilia said coolly. "No attention was required. The story was everywhere. You're fairly ubiquitous these days, aren't you?"

"If by ubiquitous you mean wealthy and powerful, I accept the description proudly."

"Because that's what matters to you." She couldn't seem to help herself. Because she had to keep poking and poking to make sure that he really was this stranger he'd turned into. That the man she'd thought he was had never been anything but a figment of her own imagination. She had to be *certain*. "Money at all costs. No matter who it hurts."

"Who does it hurt?" His gaze was far too bright. Particularly with his mouth set in that harsh line. "There will always be rich men, Cecilia. Why shouldn't I be one of them?"

"I think the real question is why you're here," she said past the lump in her throat for the man she'd nursed all those weeks. The man she'd believed was different. The man who had never existed, not really. "Because I want to be clear about something, Pascal. We like this valley quiet. Remote. The sisters spend their lives here engaged in quiet contemplation. If they want the bustle of the city, they know how to drive themselves down to Verona. What none of us need or want, villager and nun alike, is whatever scheming Roman nonsense you or your minions brought with you."

"I told you." And his voice was harsher then. "I came here to face a ghost, nothing more."

"I know that ghost is not me. Perhaps the ghost is the man you were, when you were here before. Because if we're being honest, you left *him* that night, too."

He didn't flinch. He didn't reel away from her as if she'd hit him. And yet, somehow, Cecilia had the distinct impression that she'd landed a blow. Possibly with a very sharp knife.

And she would have to spend some time questioning herself later. She would have to try to figure out why, when she'd dreamed of landing blow after blow, each harder than the last, the doing of it made her feel shaken.

"But that is something you can sort out on your own," she said, hoping she didn't sound as off balance as she felt. "It doesn't involve me."

Because if she stood here any longer, she would forget herself. And she already knew what happened when she allowed herself to *forget*, particularly when she was around Pascal. More to the point, her life was different now. She had no desire to change it completely. Not anymore. Not again.

She stepped around him, yanking her bucket off the floor as she went. She headed for the door at the side of the altar that led into the vestry, thinking she could bar herself in the church if necessary. There were hours yet before she was due to pick up Dante and she very much doubted that a man like Pascal would lounge around, waiting. Whatever whim had brought him here would have him bored silly and heading for home before long.

"Cecilia."

And she hated herself, because his voice, her name, stopped her. He still had that power over her. She had the despairing notion he always would.

"I'm going now," she said, glaring at the window up above her. "Whatever you wanted out of this sudden return is your business. But I don't want it. I don't want any part of it."

"You said I couldn't *have him*," he said. "Tell me who he is."

She was staring up at the stained glass before her. And this was the moment of truth, wasn't it? She had tried to call, of course. Once he had started appearing on the news, and in the magazines. She tried to do her duty by him. But she'd never made it past the main switchboard of his company. No matter who she spoke to, and no matter how they promised that someone would get back to her if her claim was found to be worthy, no one ever did.

Three years in, she'd stopped trying.

Since then she'd been certain that given the chance, she would, of course, come clean at the first opportunity.

But she hadn't.

She'd excused the fact she hadn't made the situation clear to his board members. She'd told herself that they didn't deserve to know something Pascal didn't already know himself. But deep down she'd believed that she would never see him again. That this moment would never come.

Now he was here. She had foolishly thrown Dante in his face straight off. Now he'd asked directly.

It was another opportunity to discover who she was, and once more Cecilia was faced with the lowering notion that it was not who she'd thought. Not at all. Because she wanted—more than anything—to lie. To say whatever was necessary to make him let her go. Forget about her. And never, ever, get anywhere near Dante.

She squeezed her eyes shut. She was too aware of her own pulse, pounding in places it normally didn't. She swallowed, not surprised to find her throat was dry.

And then she made herself turn, because she had done harder things than this. Like sit up in a bed in the clinic, without a stitch of clothing on her body, and face Mother Superior directly. Then explain what on earth she was doing there. Or like when she'd started to show, and had been forced to leave the abbey—the only home she'd ever known—and find her own cottage to live in, just her and her growing belly and her eternal shame.

And neither of those things was all that difficult stood next to childbirth.

So she faced him. The man she had loved, hated and lost either way.

And she had no optimism whatsoever that what she was about to tell him would change that.

In fact, she suspected she was about to make it all much worse.

"*He* is your son," she said, her voice echoing in the otherwise empty church. "His name is Dante. He doesn't know you exist. And no, before you ask, I have absolutely no intention of changing that."

CHAPTER THREE

HER WORDS WERE IMPOSSIBLE.

They made no sense, no matter how loudly they echoed in his head.

Pascal thought perhaps he staggered back beneath the weight of all that impossibility, possibly even crumpled to the floor—but of course, he did no such thing. He was frozen into place as surely as if the stones beneath him had made him a statue, staring back at her.

In horror. In confusion.

There must be some mistake, a sliver of rationality deep inside him insisted.

"What did you say?" he managed to ask through a mouth that no longer felt like his own.

Because while he was certain he had heard her perfectly well, no matter how he tried to rearrange those words in his head, they still didn't make sense. They couldn't make sense.

"This isn't something I *want* to tell you," Cecilia said, tilting her chin up in a belligerent sort of way that was one more thing that didn't make sense.

Because the sweet almost-nun he'd known hadn't had the faintest hint of belligerence in her entire body. Though her body was obviously the last thing in the world he needed to be thinking about just now.

"It's the right thing to do," she was saying. "So. Now you know."

And then, astonishingly, nodded in punctuation. As if the subject was now closed.

"I cannot be understanding you." His voice sounded as little like his own as the words felt in his mouth, and he still couldn't seem to move the way he wanted to. Or at all.

Cecilia sighed as if he was testing her patience, another affront to add to the list. "You have a son, Pascal. And you shouldn't be surprised to hear that. If memory serves, you never spared the slightest thought for any kind of birth control. What did you think would happen?"

It was the sheer insult of that—and the unfairness—that seared through him, hot enough to loosen his paralysis.

"I was recovering from a car accident in a hospital," he gritted out. "When do you imagine I might have nipped out to the shops and found appropriate protection? I assumed you had taken care of it."

"Taken care of it?" She actually laughed, which nearly let Pascal's temper get the better of him. But she didn't seem to notice. Or care if she did. "I was raised in a convent. With real-life, actual nuns. It might surprise you to learn that the finer details of condom use during premarital sex didn't come up much during morning prayers."

Pascal dragged his hands through his hair, though it was cut almost too short to allow it. Unless he was very much mistaken, his hands were actually shaking, something that might have horrified him unto his soul at any other moment. But right now he could hardly do more than note it and move on. It was that or succumb to the high tide swamping him, drowning him, tugging him violently out to sea.

"I cannot have a son," he snapped out, not caring that his words were far too angry for a place like this. Holy and quiet, with the watchful eyes of too many saints upon him—and none of them as sharp as Cecilia's gaze. "I cannot."

Cecilia sniffed. And her remarkable eyes sparked with what he thought was temper, however little that made sense to him.

"And yet you do. But don't worry. He's perfect, and he doesn't need you." The gleam in her eyes intensified, and he felt it like a blow to the center of his chest. "Feel free to run back to your glossy magazines. Your lingerie models. Whatever makes you happy, Pascal. You can pretend we don't exist. The way you've been doing for six years."

"How dare you take that tone with me." His voice was soft, because his fury was so intense he thought it might have singed his vocal cords. The rage and grief in him so hot and blistering he wasn't sure he'd ever speak in a normal voice again. "You never told me you were pregnant."

"How would I have done that?" She fired the question at him, plunking her bucket back down on the stone floor with a loud crash. She even took a step toward him as if she wanted this confrontation to get physical. "The first time I saw you mentioned in the papers, two years had gone by. Before that? You'd just disappeared overnight. The army had discharged you, and even if they hadn't, they weren't about to hand out a forwarding address. What was I supposed to have done?"

"You knew I was from Rome. You knew—"

If he hadn't been close enough to see the pulse in her neck go wild, he might have believed the cold smile she aimed at him meant she wasn't affected by this interaction. But Pascal wasn't sure that knowledge was helpful.

"Right. So you think I should have…what? Wandered up and down the Spanish Steps while heavily pregnant?" she demanded. "Calling out your name? Or better still, climbed atop the Trevi Fountain with a newborn in my arms, demanding that someone in the crowd take me to you? How do think that would have worked?"

That she had a point only made his anguish worse.

How could this have happened? He couldn't accept it. He couldn't believe it. He wanted to tear down this godforsaken church with his hands as if that would change the way she was looking at him. As if it could turn back time.

As if that could save him from the nasty reality that he'd become exactly what he most loathed without knowing it.

"You keep mentioning magazines, which means you clearly saw me in one," he found himself saying as if he could argue the conviction from her face. As if he could make this her fault and make it better, or different, by shrugging off the blame. "You must have known the company existed. That must mean you *could have* contacted me. You obviously chose not to do so."

Her laugh sliced into him. "I called your company repeatedly. Oddly enough, no one took me seriously. Or I assume they didn't, because it took you all this time to turn up here."

"Whoever else might have turned you away will be dealt with." Though even as he said that, he already knew what had likely happened. Any reports of pregnancies would have been dismissed by Guglielmo as opportunists attempting to cash in on Pascal's success. He would never have dreamed of wasting Pascal's time with empty claims. "But if you had actually turned up on my doorstep, Cecilia, *I* would not have denied you entry."

She actually dared roll her eyes. At him. "That's good to know. Should you impregnate me and leave me behind like so much trash again, I'll be sure to take that tack. I'll gather up whatever children you've abandoned, camp out in your lobby and hope for the best. What could possibly go wrong?"

"What kind of person has a man's child and fails to tell him?" Something cracked wide open inside him, and it was harder and harder to pretend he was *angry* when it went far deeper than that. When it felt like a catastrophic fissure, deep within. "It has been *six years*. Do you have any idea what you've done?"

"I know exactly what I've done, because I've been here the whole time, doing it," she fired back at him, and he had the uneasy notion that she could see that yawning expanse inside him and was aiming straight for it. For him. "You knew where I was. You knew that I was unpardonably naive. You weren't without experience as you made a point of mentioning more than once. Surely you must have known that anytime people have sex, especially without any protection, there's the possibility of exactly this occurring. You never inquired."

"How dare you put this responsibility on me."

"I will not stand here and listen to lectures from the likes of you on *responsibility*, thank you," she bit out. She moved even closer then, and went so far as to jab a finger toward him—very much as if she'd have liked to put out his eye. "You try being a single parent. All the feedings and diaper changes, the cry-ing for no reason and sudden, scary illnesses. Where were you? Not here, handling them."

"I could hardly handle something I didn't know was happening."

She jabbed that finger again, and it occurred to Pascal that she wasn't the least bit intimidated by him. He couldn't recall the last time he'd encountered such a thing. And certainly not from a woman he'd thought was a ghost a few hours ago—and who he remembered as nothing but sweet.

"Don't misunderstand me," she was saying with more than a little ferocity. "There's more joy in it than ought to be possible, or the species would have died out. But what *I'm* talking about is keeping a tiny human alive. What *you're* talking about is your own hurt feelings because you chose to disappear into the ether and it turns out, there are consequences for that. One of them is the child you helped make."

He felt pale with that anguish, mixed liberally with fury. "You dare to speak to me of consequences?"

"I've lived your consequences, Pascal," Cecilia retorted. "An absolutely marvelous little boy has grown into a five-year-old as a consequence of your carelessness. And after trying more than enough times, I didn't keep banging my head against brick walls trying to find a man who didn't leave behind so much as a telephone number. I decided that I was going to focus my attention on raising my son, instead. And did."

"Cecilia—"

"I never expected you to show your face here again," she told him. "I don't expect you to stay now. You're acting as if knowing I was pregnant would have changed something, but I'll let you in on a secret, Pascal. I know full well it wouldn't have. Why don't you spare us both the dramatics and just…go away again?"

Pascal really did stagger then. He had to reach out to keep himself upright, gripping the back of the nearest pew.

As if her certainty that he would abandon his own child no matter the circumstances was almost as grave a betrayal as the fact she'd kept this secret so long.

"I told you," he said, too many memories flooding his brain then. Of the hours she'd spent at his bedside, talking as well as tending to him. All the things he'd told her in return, because his bed in that clinic had felt disconnected to the world. Why not tell a kind stranger every feeling that had ever moved in him? Why not share every story he had inside him? He'd done that and more. How could she imagine that the man who had done so would turn around and leave now? "I told you how I was raised. What it meant to me to be a bastard son to a cruel, unfeeling man… Have you forgotten?"

Her eyes seemed nearly purple then, with what he only hoped was distress. "I didn't forget. But people say all kinds of things when they think their lives might end, then turn around and *live* very differently, when given the chance."

"I told you," Pascal growled. "And you decided to do this to me anyway. To my child. When you had to know it was the last thing I would ever have allowed."

Whatever distress might have been lurking in her, it disappeared in a flush of temper as her chin tipped up again.

"I stopped caring about what you might or might not allow," she said with a distinct calm that felt like yet another slap when he could barely keep himself together. "Right about the time it became clear to me that you weren't coming back, and that I was really, truly going to have to have our baby all on my own. And then carry on raising him. I considered adoption, you know. Because my plan was to be a nun, not a mother." Her tone was bitter then. "Never a mother."

Something tickled at the back of his mind, about Cecilia's stories about her own childhood, but he thrust it aside. Because she'd actually wanted to...

"You wanted to give up your child—*my* child?"

Once again Pascal couldn't force his mind to process that. He couldn't seem to breathe past it. It was bad enough that he'd come here on a whim to discover that all this time, the woman who'd haunted him through his life in Rome had kept his child a secret from him. But that he could have come back here today, just like this, and never know? Never have the slightest notion what he'd lost?

That fissure inside him widened. And grew teeth.

"Yes, Pascal," she said. Because she had teeth, too. And they seemed to sharpen by the second. "It was never my intention to have a child on my own. Why *wouldn't* I consider adoption?"

Again Pascal ran a hand over his jaw, his scars. Reminding himself that he had survived the impossible before. Surely he would again.

One way or another.

"I suppose you would like me to thank you for choosing motherhood," he said, unable to keep the bitterness from his voice. "I find I cannot quite get there. I want to see him."

He wasn't looking at her as he said that, and it took him a moment to realize she hadn't responded. When he slid his gaze back to hers, she had a considering sort of look on her face. As if she was mulling over a decision as she looked at him.

For the first time it occurred to Pascal that she might very well bar him from seeing the child. *His* child.

How could he be outraged at being denied something he hadn't known he had when he'd driven into this valley? How could he know himself so little?

"I'll show you a photograph," Cecilia replied, her violet eyes glittering with more of that same *consideration*. "I'm certainly not introducing you to him. He's five. As far as he's aware, he doesn't have a father."

Pascal blinked, but once more couldn't really take that in. He felt drunk again, as reckless and out of control as he'd been when he'd driven that car over the side of a mountain. This was like living through that crash again and again. And more, he felt broken into a thousand pieces, the way he had then.

He reminded himself that he was the president and CEO of an international corporation that had made him a billionaire. He laughed off deals that would make other men sweat. He could surely handle one parochial woman and the rest of this…situation.

All he needed to do was stop letting his damned feelings dictate his reactions.

Something he'd thought he'd stamped out years ago. Six years ago, in fact, when he'd received the ultimate wake-up call, had remembered himself and had left.

Cut his own feelings about his father out of this and it was a fairly simple thing. She hadn't been able to track him down. He hadn't looked back. It wasn't even a saga—it was depressingly common.

He cleared his throat. "So you…live here. With him. At the abbey?"

"We have our own cottage," she said. Grudgingly, he thought.

And Pascal felt better now that he'd allowed a bit of reason back into the mix. More like himself and less like the broken man she'd known.

He looked at the bucket beside her. "If you do

not live in the abbey, and you are not a nun or even a novitiate any longer, why on earth are you cleaning this church?"

"I clean," she said. And when he stared back at her without comprehension, she lifted her pugilistic little chin again. The expression on her face was challenging, which he should probably stop finding so surprising. "That's what I do. For a living."

"You...clean. For a living. This is how you support yourself?"

"That's what I said."

This time he understood her completely. The words did not bloom into that same dull roar in his head. He felt like himself again, and that allowed him the comfort of the sort of temper he recognized. Not the volcanic, tectonic shift of before—but the sort of laser focus he usually saved for creatures like his father.

Fewer feelings. More fury.

He liked this version of himself much better.

"Are you truly this vindictive?" he asked her, his voice soft with menace and the power he'd fought for—and had no intention of ceding to a fallen nun, thank you. He shifted his position to shove his hands into his pockets and kept his gaze trained on her. "You say you read about me. You knew about the company and claim you called. So there can be no debate about the fact that you know perfectly well that I'm not a poor man. That no matter what else happened, I would never willingly consign my child to be raised in poverty."

Color bloomed in her cheeks, and he had the sense it was the first honest response he'd seen from her. Maybe that was why he reveled in it, like a thirsty man faced with a mountain spring.

Surely there could be no other reason.

"Your child is not being raised in poverty," she snapped. "He doesn't take a private jet to get his shopping done, I grant you, but his life is full. He wants for nothing. And I'm sorry that you think cleaning is beneath you, but luckily, I don't. I make a good living. I take care of myself and my son. Not everybody needs to be rich."

"Not everyone can be rich, it is true. But you happen to be raising the son and heir of a man who is. Several times over."

"Money only buys *things*, Pascal," she said with the dismissiveness of someone who had never lived more or less by their wits in the worst parts of a major city. "It certainly doesn't make a person happy. As anyone who looks at you can tell quite clearly."

"How would you know?" he asked, his tone deadly.

She flushed again. "I make Dante perfectly happy. That's what matters."

"You live in the middle of nowhere, surrounded by nothing but cows and nuns. What kind of life is this for a boy?"

"There was a time when you thought this valley was paradise," she threw at him. "It hasn't changed any. But if you have, there is no need for you to suffer the cows and the nuns a moment more. You can turn around and leave right now."

"I don't think you're understanding me." He sounded almost gentle, he noted, which was at odds with that cold fury inside him. He leaned into it, because it was better than that terrible fissure. "I am Pascal Furlani and we are discussing the sole heir to everything I have built. No son and heir of mine can grow up like this, so far away from everything that matters."

She scowled. "Then it's a lucky thing your name isn't on his birth certificate, isn't it? You don't have to worry yourself about how he's raised."

Pascal couldn't seem to do anything but stay frozen solid where he stood, staring at her as if, were he to focus, he could make this go away. He could turn her into the ghost she should have been, not... *this*. Not mother to another bastard child, but this one his. *His.*

The scandal when it was discovered—because these things were always discovered, as Pascal knew all too well himself—would brand him the worst kind of hypocrite, given he'd never made any secret of his feelings on his own father's behavior. He'd made himself the asterisk forever attached to his father's name.

Now he would have his own, and he knew full well the tabloids would have a field day with him.

But the thought of scandal made a different sort of apprehension grip him.

"Did you tell the members of my board about this child?" he demanded.

"I didn't want to tell *you* about this child," she replied furiously, her scowl deepening. "So no, I didn't share the news with two complete strangers marching around the village officiously, asking rude questions."

"But that doesn't mean they couldn't have seen you. Or have asked someone else. Or otherwise figured it out."

"I didn't much care what they did." And now she sounded impatient, which was just one more insult to add to the pile. "Just so long as they left. Which I would also like you to do. Now."

Pascal couldn't let himself think directly about the child. *His* child. His *son*. It was too much. It was so heavy he was convinced it would flatten him—but thinking about his spiteful, grasping board members in possession of this secret he hadn't known he was keeping was different. It was easier to think about what they would do with the information than it was to think about the information itself.

Or that *the information* was a little boy who didn't know he had a father who would never, ever have abandoned him if he'd had the choice.

"This is a disaster," he muttered, more to himself than to her.

But she heard him. Maybe he'd wanted her to hear him.

"Funnily enough, that's what I thought you would say." Her scowl smoothed out and her chin went up as if she was wrapping herself in armor. "As a matter of fact, all of this is happening precisely the way I imagined it would. So why don't we fast-forward to the inevitable end without all of this carrying on that won't get us anywhere?" Her violet eyes flashed as they held his gaze. "Just go. Leave here and return to your money and your life in Rome. No one has to know that you ever came here. Dante and I will muddle along as we always have and you can spend your time however it is you like. No harm, no foul."

And she even waved her hand through the air with a languid indifference that made something in Pascal simply…snap.

One moment he was standing frozen and still in his fury, and the next he had moved toward her. He wrapped his hands around her soft, narrow shoulders, then held her there before him.

Cecilia made a slight startled sound. Her hands came up and she braced her fingers against his abdomen, though she didn't push him away or try to pull back from him. It was as if she was holding her breath, waiting to see what he would do.

But all he did was lower his face so it was directly in hers.

"This is not going to go away," he promised her, a thundering thing in his voice, though he kept it low. Even. "I am not going to go away. I have a son. *A son.* You have made me a father and taken it away from me, and I will never forgive you for either one of those things. But I know now. And nothing will be the same. Do you understand me?"

He expected her to order him to let go of her, which he would do, of course, because he wasn't the animal she seemed to think he was. Even if it wasn't exactly lost on him that even now, even with what he knew, his body was having a far more enthusiastic reaction to the close proximity with the woman who had haunted him all these years. Her shoulders fit perfectly in his palms, as ever.

And the last time he'd been this close to her, it had been a prelude to his mouth on hers. Then the hardest part of him deep inside her melting, clenching heat, making them both ache. Then shatter. Then do it all over again.

"That," she said very distinctly, her violet eyes wide and fixed to his, "is absolutely never happening again."

For the first time since he'd walked into this church, he saw the woman he'd left here six years ago. The one who had always known what he was thinking. The one who had so often been thinking the very same thing.

She certainly was now.

And she had kept this secret from him. She had made him into his worst nightmare. Pascal wanted to crush her. He wanted to cry. He wanted to tear apart this church and rip this whole valley apart with his hands. He wanted to rage hard enough to turn back time, so that he could prevent this tragedy from happening in the first place.

Or, something far more insidious whispered inside him, *so you could stay this time. The way you wanted to back then.*

And that thought was the biggest betrayal of them all.

Because staying here had never been an option, no matter how much he'd wanted it once. And no matter what price it turned out he'd have to pay for going.

Pascal stopped fighting that roar inside him. He surrendered to the yawning thing, rage and grief, fury and need.

He had never forgotten Cecilia Reginald. He had come back here to exorcise her, but now it seemed he would be twined with her forever in the son they'd made.

It was too much.

It was all *too much*.

So he hauled her up onto her toes and brought her even closer to him, then crushed his mouth to hers.

CHAPTER FOUR

HIS KISS WAS MUCH, much, much worse than she remembered.

It was hotter. Wilder.

Better, something in her cried.

But this time she knew how to kiss him back.

He had taught her. Six years ago he had taught her how to light the world on fire. How to burn so hot and so bright that she hadn't much cared if he was turning her to ash in his wake—she'd wanted only to keep getting too close to the flames.

Cecilia would have sworn that she couldn't remember any of it. A moment ago she'd have been certain that all those memories had been swept away in the trials and joys of motherhood. That it was all dim recollections of warmth and nothing more.

But it turned out, she remembered everything.

She remembered his taste, and the way he cupped the back of her head with one big, hard palm, guiding her where and how he liked. She remembered the wildfire that scared her and excited her in turn, roaring through her and lighting her up. Everywhere.

She remembered how to angle her head. How to move closer. How to press her body against his until she was all fire again. Fire and need, passion and desire.

Kissing him was like traveling back in time.

She remembered her own innocence. How she'd given it to him, and how carefully, how gently, he had taken it and made her sob with joy and wonder.

She remembered the first time he had kissed her, there in that whitewashed room where he'd spent his convalescence. How he'd pressed his lips to hers, smiling as he'd coaxed her. Taught her. Then tempted her beyond endurance.

She had always imagined, before then, that a kiss would take something from her. And over the past six years she'd told herself rather darkly that she'd been all too right about that. But the truth she'd forgotten—or she'd made herself forget—was that his kiss had made her feel…bigger. Better. Brighter and more powerful than she had ever been before. Like some kind of shooting star.

Here, now, was no different.

She could feel herself shooting wild across a dark night sky, lighting up the world with the force of her longing.

He kissed her, and she kissed him back as if she'd been waiting all this time for him to come back. As if she'd *wanted* this. And with every scrape of his tongue against hers, she felt that same light. That heat.

Cecilia did the only thing she could. She poured all her lost hope, all her misery and worry, anxiety and loneliness, into the way she kissed him back. She kissed him with all the pride she'd stored up inside her for the little boy he'd never known. The love and the odd moments of gratitude that Pascal had come into her life and left her the greatest gift, no matter the cost.

Everything he'd missed. Everything she'd wished for. She kissed him and she kissed him; she poured it all into him, and got passion in return.

Passion and intensity. Greed and delight.

His hands moved, tracing their way down her back as if he was reacquainting himself with her shape. Her strength.

She shifted, her palms moving down the front of his shirt to find him harder. More solid. And even hotter than she'd let herself recall. It wasn't until she found her way to his belt buckle that she remembered where they were.

Not just in this valley, not far from the abbey that had been her childhood home and where she would never, now, be the nun she'd always imagined she would.

More than that, they were standing in the church where she'd learned how to pray.

She was defiling herself all over again.

Cecilia wrenched herself back, tearing her mouth from his and pushing against his wall of a chest with her hands. But he was so much bigger and tougher than he had been six years ago, and she only managed to create about a centimeter of space between them.

Still, it was enough for reality to charge in and horrify her.

"That will never happen again," she managed to say.

She thought he would laugh, or say something arrogant and cutting. But all Pascal did was gaze down at her, an odd expression on his starkly beautiful face.

"I'm not so certain," he said after a moment.

She pushed against him again, and this time he let her go. And she didn't have it in her to explore the reasons why that made her heart clench. She felt the end of the pew behind her and gripped it. As if anchoring herself here could save her. As if she hadn't blasphemed in every possible way.

Again.

When she knew better.

"Thank you for reminding me that the chemistry between us is dangerous and upsetting," she said, and she made herself meet his gaze when it was the last thing she wanted to do. "It leads nowhere I want to go."

"I had convinced myself I'd imagined it," he said. And she might have taken offense at that if he hadn't sounded so…disgruntled. "I told myself I was weak. Out of my head with pain and recovery and healing. That was the only explanation that made sense."

He lifted his hand to his face, but this time, instead of running his fingers over his scars, he ran them over his mouth. Which reminded Cecilia that she could taste him on her tongue.

Damn him. And damn her for surrendering so easily once more.

Pascal was still studying her as if she'd turned into a creature he couldn't name, right there before his eyes. "But it turns out you're more potent than I gave you credit for."

"I do not wish to be potent," Cecilia managed to get out. "And I do not want any credit. What I want is for you to forget me. The way you already have, for years, before you came back here."

That mouth of his twisted. "But that's the trouble, *cara*. I did not forget."

Cecilia hated this. Him. And most of all, herself.

Because she should have been better prepared for something like this. She'd been on edge when those other men had come and sniffed around the abbey asking questions about Pascal Furlani's famous car accident, but she hadn't really believed that Pascal himself would follow. She'd assumed that if he sent anyone else, it would be more emissaries of the officious variety. Attorneys, she'd supposed, to make her sign documents that would renounce any claim to him she might have had. She'd been ready for that. She prepared stinging speeches that she could deliver to his men, making it clear that she wanted nothing from him and never had and never would.

She hadn't expected him.

And she certainly hadn't expected that he would kiss her again.

Because it cut the knees straight out of her argument, not to mention all her prepared rebukes. It reminded her too well of the reasons she'd given up everything she knew for him.

The truth was, it had been years since she could even imagine how it was that she'd allowed a torn-up soldier to turn her from her chosen path so easily. Sometimes she would sit up at night, when Dante was sound asleep and looked angelic, instead of the whirl of holy terror and inexhaustible energy he could be when he was awake. She would gaze at him, allowing herself to feel that flood of maternal love—but still completely unable to understand how it all happened.

How had a person as quiet and contained as she was...do what she did?

Her life had been divided into before Pascal and after him, and the further she got away from those stolen months, the less he seemed real in her memories. There were a thousand stories about the fecklessness of youth, after all. Everyone knew that

young girls were easy pickings, and as embarrass-
ing as it might have been for Cecilia to think of herself in that way, that was the story she'd accepted
about herself. That was the story she told, when it
was necessary to tell it at all, here in a small valley
filled with people who had known her since the day
she'd arrived here and could tell her story for her.
And often did.

It was a hard shock to discover that all she'd done
was mute the man.

Because the reality of Pascal was in full, living
color. And his kiss was electrifying.

And Cecilia understood that she'd been lying to
herself for a long, long time.

She found she didn't know quite how to process
any of that.

"This is all irrelevant," she said now. She moved
away from him, aware that her body no longer felt
like her own. That irritated her almost more than the
rest, because it had taken her so long to get it back.
There had been Pascal, then Dante, and years before she'd become simply *Cecilia* again. "Feel free to
send your lawyers. Do your worst. I can't say I care."

"Lawyers?" He sounded mystified, though she
didn't look back at him to see. "What do my lawyers
have to do with anything?"

"Rich men are renowned for going to great
lengths to make sure they don't have to give away

any of their money, for any reason. Call it what you like. I'm not going to fight you."

"I'm not following you." And his voice changed as he said that. Less the man as surprised as she was at the way that kiss had exploded between them and more…dangerous. It sent a shiver down her spine. Because suddenly, she had no trouble imagining him as a leader of men. A captain of his industry in every regard. "Was I planning to give away my money in some capacity?"

"I'm sure you'll have a battalion of documents for me to sign. So you don't have to claim Dante. And so I will never make any kind of claim on you. Whatever. What I'm trying to say is that I expect it."

"Cecilia." Her name was like an oath. "There is no circumstance under which I would knowingly renounce my claim to my own child. Understand this now."

She couldn't help but look back at him then, though she instantly wished she hadn't. There was an intensity in Pascal's black-gold gaze that made her clench her teeth tight to hold back the shudder that threatened to take her over.

But all that did was send all that sensation spiraling down through her body until it lodged low in her belly.

"You say that now." She told herself he couldn't see her reaction to him. That all she had to do was pretend she wasn't having one. "I think it's likely the shock. Once it wears off you'll change your tune. You'll want nothing more than to get back to your preferred life."

"This is what you think of me?" His voice was quiet, but she didn't mistake it for weakness. Not when it seemed to fill the small church, swelling up from the stones at her feet. "You concealed my own child from me for all these years. Now you imagine that having learned of him at last, I will abandon him all over again. This from a woman who spent months sitting at my bedside. Talking to me. Getting to know me in some small way, I would have thought."

That pricked at her. "The man I thought I knew would never have left the way you did, in the dark of night. With no word."

Pascal didn't move toward her, so there was no reason she should have felt as if he loomed over her, trapping her, when she'd put several pews between them.

"Remind me, whose hurt feelings are at play here?" he asked in that same quiet way that hummed in her, intense and demanding. "Mine, because of the consequences of my actions? Or yours, because you feel slighted by a choice that might have had to do with you, but you must have known full well had nothing to do with the child."

"It doesn't matter whose feelings are hurt," she fired back, stung. And something like terrified that he'd hit on something she hadn't even known was inside her. Was she truly so petty? It made her stomach hurt that she couldn't immediately answer in the negative. "What matters is that I don't intend to allow my child to play victim to your periodic sentimentality."

He let out a harsh sound. "I have no idea what that means."

"You can't possibly want him," Cecilia said, exasperated.

She had the sense of him growing bigger again. Sharper, this time. Like a loaded weapon, pointed straight at her.

"You do not have the slightest idea what it is I want," he said in that same deadly tone. "How can you, when I hardly know myself? You have known about this child's existence for the past six years. I have known about it for thirty minutes. Pray, do not tell me what it is I *want* when I am still reacting to the news that this child exists."

"I don't want Dante to have to pay for it while you sort through your emotions."

"Cecilia. You do not get to decide what and how I feel about any of this. And you certainly will not dictate what I do."

She didn't mistake that for anything but the threat it was.

"This isn't one of your boardrooms, Pascal," she threw at him. "He's *my* child. You don't get to rip open his life unless I say you can, and I say you absolutely can't."

Pascal laughed. But it was not a sound of amusement.

Cecilia felt it like a kick to the gut.

"You should never have kept my son from me all this time, but you did," he told her, his voice as dark as his gaze, and that thunderous expression he wore. "We all get to do what we can get away with, don't we? And now that I know about him, there is nothing that will keep me from him. And you should know that there is very little I can't get away with, *cara*."

"Stop threatening me!" she snapped at him.

He laughed again, and it was not exactly soothing. "I have yet to begin threatening you."

She panicked. There was no other way to put it. She wasn't sure she could feel the top of her head; her lips still throbbed, she could *taste* him and he showed no sign whatsoever of slowing down.

"Who's to say he even is your child?" she heard herself ask as if the stained-glass saints could answer for her. Or help her out of this situation. "Your name is nowhere on his birth certificate. He might as well have been delivered by fairies for all you have to do with it."

Pascal looked wholly unperturbed. "Then you really will meet my lawyers, when they arrive here *en masse* to demand and perform a DNA test. Do you really want to force me to force this issue? Because I will. Happily."

What Cecilia wanted to do was scream at him. Rail against him until she satisfied all those hurt feelings inside her that he'd pointed out and that she couldn't pretend weren't there any longer. Until she made him pay, somehow, for all these years and all her loneliness and all she'd lost—

But that was about her. And this needed to be about Dante.

"Listen to me," she said, and she didn't care if he could hear all that emotion in her voice. She wanted him to hear it. She wanted him to understand this, if nothing else. "Dante is a happy, healthy little boy. But this is his whole life. This valley. Me, his mother and only parent. He has yet to so much as question me about whether or not he has a father."

"Do you truly expect that to last? You cannot be so naive."

The fact that she had, on some level, expected it to be a non-issue because she wanted it that way struck her as unbearably foolish then. Something more sinister than simply *naive*. It was one more ugly part of herself she would have to pull out and look at closely—but not now. Not where he could witness all the ways he'd knocked her off her foundations today.

"You barreling into his life and claiming him as your child when that is meaningless to him can only hurt him," she made herself say in as steady a voice as she could manage, under the circumstances. "It will confuse him terribly and I don't want that. And if you're serious about wanting to take your place as some kind of father to him, you shouldn't want it, either."

And for a moment the church was quiet. Pascal kept his dark gaze on her, stern and accusatory, but he didn't speak. Cecilia watched a muscle in his lean cheek flex as if he was biting back his own strong emotions.

The light changed outside, sending the colors from the windows dancing over him, and something shuddered through her, too much like foreboding. She knew, like some kind of terrible premonition, that he meant what he said. That he wanted to be a part of his son's life after all. That she had kept a child from a father who would have wanted him, not the careless, reckless liar she'd thought he was.

And that was a possibility she had never prepared herself for.

It made her feel sick.

"Whatever you do," she said, though it felt like a kind of surrender, "I beg you, do not toy with my son's emotions for the sake of your own ego. Please, Pascal."

But when the tension between them roared into a higher gear, she understood that somehow, her plea had made it all worse.

"I can understand that you're not expecting me,"

he bit out with a furious, exacting note in his voice that sounded to her like pure condemnation. "And I can even understand that you perhaps require some time to prepare him for this. But my patience is finite, Cecilia. And I am not leaving this valley until I not only meet my son, but also claim him—formally—as my own. I'm prepared to stay as long as necessary to make that happen."

Too many things whirled around in her head at once then. Too many questions—and too much fear. What would happen if he claimed Dante, formally or otherwise? Would they turn into one more modern version of unconnected parents, forever shipping him off from one place to the other? Would Dante grow up without a sense of his own real home—which had always been one of the great comforts of Cecilia's own life? How would she survive a life that included huge swathes of time without her own son?

She wanted no part of any of that. But she gulped down the questions that threatened to bubble over from inside her, because she was terribly afraid they would come out as tears. And that was the final, ultimate humiliation. She wouldn't—couldn't—allow it. It would break her.

And Cecilia refused to let him break her. Not this time. Not again.

"I hope you enjoy camping alfresco, then," she said instead, heading toward the door. "The *pensione* is closed this time of year. And you're certainly not welcome to stay with me."

She shot a look over her shoulder at him when she reached the door, because she was so damnably weak, and something caught at her. Pascal stood where she'd left him, so solitary, and yet so *sure*. As if he were a pillar that held up the world, or at least this church, and could stand like that forever.

He will, something in her whispered, making goose bumps break out all over her skin. *You will never be rid of him again.*

"Alternatively, you can always throw yourself on the mercy of the nuns," she threw at him, hoping her desperation didn't show on her face. Yet somehow sure that it did. "I'm sure they remember you all too well. But no worries. They took vows. If you ask them for sanctuary, I believe they're duty bound to take you in."

With that, Cecilia threw open the door to the vestry and escaped from her past. But she knew, even as she slammed the heavy door behind her and collapsed against it, that it was only temporary.

And there was no one to help her or save her now as it tightened around her throat and pulled tight, like a noose.

CHAPTER FIVE

"WE ARE NOT in the habit of turning away petitioners in need," said Mother Superior, her face as smooth and ageless as it had been six years ago. She could have been fifty or eighty, for all Pascal could tell. There was a canny wisdom in her gaze and a certain scratchy archness in her voice. And the smile she aimed at him made him want to drop to his knees and rededicate himself to a faith he had never felt deeply enough to pronounce in the first place. "Not even those who took advantage of our hospitality once before."

"You are too good," Pascal murmured in reply.

He would sooner rip off his own arms than admit how strange it had seemed to him to walk up to the front door of the abbey. Then wait to be admitted into Mother Superior's presence as if he was any visitor. Not one who had lived here for months and not of his own accord.

Pascal had never intended to return.

Moreover, he had gone to great lengths to deny

that he had ever been as helpless or weak as he had been when he'd been stuck here. He liked to touch his scars to remind him that he could overcome any obstacle, but he had stopped permitting himself to remember the details of this particular obstacle. This valley and the stone abbey were a story he told to illustrate both his strength of will and his ability to climb out of any pit.

He'd managed to convince himself that none of it was real.

But the stone building that housed the abbey had stood in this same spot for centuries. It had been a fortress, a castle and a monastery, and it was built to last ten more centuries in much the same forbidding condition. He followed Mother Superior as she glided along the smooth, spotless halls, made somewhat less dim by the lights set into sconces every few meters. He had to double-check that the lights were electric, and not torches. Because otherwise, it could have been any one of the past five centuries.

It was a relief to exit the old part of the abbey and cross into the modern clinic building. And somehow he was not the least bit surprised when the nun led him to the very same chamber where he'd stayed years before. He stopped in the doorway, not sure he was in complete control of himself as he looked around. But nothing had changed. The same whitewashed walls, free of everything save two items that were surely not considered decoration. The crucifix on the wall across from the narrow bed. And above the bed, a Bible verse in a frame.

No wonder he had spent his time staring out the window at the cold fields instead.

"As you can see, we have kept everything just as you left it," Mother Superior said genially, but her gaze was sharp.

"How thoughtful," Pascal managed to say, even as a revolt took place inside him. As if he was doomed to months of confinement if he stepped across the threshold—

But he was not a superstitious man.

And he would not let this absurd attack of malicious nostalgia affect him.

He stepped into the room, reclaiming it. Because the last time he'd been here, he'd been carried inside. In pieces.

It took him a long time to look at the nun. And to get the distinct impression she'd known exactly how hard it was for him to be here.

"Perhaps this time you can concentrate more on the cultivation of inner peace, and less on external stimulation," she said when she had his full attention, her tone dry enough to make a desert weep.

Pascal would not have taken that tone from anyone else, but this was Mother Superior. And Pascal might not consider himself one of the faithful, but he was an Italian man, and therefore entirely too

Catholic by definition to fight with a nun. No matter what she did.

Something he was certain Mother Superior knew well.

Once she left him to his uneasy memories, Pascal found himself with nothing to do but sit on the edge of the narrow bed where he'd wasted far too much time already. Most of it fighting pain and wondering if he would ever stand and walk out of this place of his own volition and on his own two feet.

And, he could admit, with a few very brief moments of joy.

All involving Cecilia.

He didn't know what impulse it had been that got him in his car and brought him here. He'd been haunted by her across the years, it was true. But he'd wanted to put that ghost to rest. He never imagined for a moment that she'd been keeping this kind of secret from him.

And it was easier to bluster on about what he wanted and what he planned to do when she was standing there in front of him.

The simple truth was that he had a son. He, Pascal Furlani, had a *son*.

He couldn't quite grasp the wonder of that. And the devastation, so quick on its heels. One chased the other, and he found himself thinking not of the little boy in the center of it, but of himself as a little boy. He had been in the center of a similar storm. And he'd found himself battered about, used as a pawn by his mother, then neglected when her machinations to force his father's hand didn't work.

He would never do that to his own child.

He vowed that to himself, here and now. Whatever happened, he would keep his feelings about what Cecilia had done in a separate compartment entirely. He would make sure that whatever the storms that raged between the two of them, the child would feel none of it. Cecilia claimed he was healthy and happy— well, now, he was healthy, happy and the sole heir to all Pascal had.

He lowered himself to prone position, and lay there, his hands folded on his chest and his eyes on the ceiling. A position he'd assumed in this very bed a thousand times before. He knew that ceiling better than he knew his own face. Every centimeter. Every faint crack or hint of discoloration. He knew how the light crept across the room on sunny days, and how the cold wind made the door rattle.

The abbey was nothing if not an excellent place for quiet contemplation of the impossible, like the existence of *his son*. Pascal stared at the ceiling and found himself wondering when he had last been somewhere that was this quiet. There were no sounds of traffic. There was no television blaring out the news. He knew there was a bell that rang out the sisters' prayers, but it wasn't ringing. And some days there were the sounds of the women who lived here, but today, the Mother Superior had told him pointedly, was a day of silence.

Pascal could hear his own heartbeat. His breath.

He had only his mobile phone, the laptop he'd left in the car and his own thoughts—which, he had to admit, was a far sight more than the last time he'd lain like this in this same bed, when he'd had only a collection of broken bones and vague assurances that he *might* make a full recovery. *Maybe.*

And this time, when he looked out the window at the cold fields that stretched toward the towering mountains, he knew that somewhere out there was a child. *His* child.

Pascal was trying to picture his son's face when he fell asleep, his body giving up after his night of driving and all the discoveries he'd made once he'd gotten here.

He woke some hours later to the insistent sound of his mobile, and scrubbed a hand over his face as he sat up, took the call and assured his secretary that he had not taken leave of his senses but was not planning to return to the office anytime soon.

His dreams had been strange and tinged with memories of that long-ago accident, which Pascal assumed was par for the course—but still irritated him.

"I will be staying up north," he managed to growl out.

"I beg your pardon?" Guglielmo replied, in mock horror. Or perhaps, the horror was not so *mock* from a deeply committed urbanite like his secretary, who had once claimed that visiting the ruins of the Roman Forum was as pastoral as he got. "You plan to *stay*? In that valley you claimed was lost in the mists of time? I'm sure I could not have heard you right. You don't mean you have returned to that abbey, do you? You hate that place!"

"Cancel my appointments," Pascal ordered him darkly. "I have things to take care of here that do not require your commentary, Guglielmo."

"This is all very mysterious, sir," his secretary replied, sounding as unfazed as ever, which was why Pascal tolerated his overfamiliarity and occasional small rebellions. "But how long do you intend to rusticate?"

"As long as it takes," Pascal told him.

It was far easier to sound certain that first day. Because he'd driven so far, then woken up in his same old bed—but he was still *him*. He hadn't woken up to discover that the last six years were all a complicated dream and he was still bedridden, weak and a nonentity with nothing to his name but a pretty novitiate who smiled too long when he looked at her.

And it wasn't until he'd ascertained that he had *not* been tossed back in time to that living nightmare that Pascal accepted how deeply he must have feared it.

That didn't sit well, so he concentrated on the present. He was here again, yes, but it wouldn't be for long. He was more than sure. Because how long could it reasonably take?

But one day passed. Then another. Pascal entertained himself with long walks around the village in the mercurial December weather, which he hadn't been able to do the last time he was here. He told himself he was content to inhale the sharp mountain air and feel winter coming in, swept down from those towering heights. He was taking his first holiday since he'd left this village on a Verona-bound bus six years ago, bound and determined to make something of himself with the second chance he'd been given.

Cecilia could take her time. He was fine.

The third day was stormy and cold. Rain pounded down in sheets outside, and being cooped up in a room that had once been his cell did not exactly improve Pascal's mood.

It became harder to convince himself that he was anything remotely resembling *fine*.

It wasn't until the fourth day—when he was storming along the same looping circle through the fields no matter the suggestion of snow in the air— that the door to a cottage set back on the road between the abbey and the village opened, and Cecilia emerged.

"Is this what you are reduced to, Pascal?" she demanded when she'd shut the door behind her and walked out toward the road. Scowling. "Are you stalking me?"

"Perhaps you have forgotten that I was incapable of taking these walks when I was last here," he told her. Perhaps too darkly. "The valley seemed larger when I could only look at it from flat on my back."

"I'm so glad we have your vote of confidence. Perhaps we can use your enthusiasm to scare up more tourism."

He eyed her, dressed similarly to how she'd been in the church. Except, he could tell instantly, those had been her work clothes. Cecilia was at home today, not prepared to clean an ancient building. She wore a dark sweater that looked sturdy and warm on her slender form. Her hair fell to her shoulders and he had the sudden, unwelcome memory of running his fingers through it as she'd lain beneath him. But what struck him most was the way the moody December sky seemed to reflect in her violet eyes, making her seem as unpredictable. Even though she'd come outside without a coat, and stood there, shivering.

But when he looked behind her to the cottage, with smoke coming out of the chimney and windows lit against the brooding afternoon, she stiffened.

"I'm not going to invite you inside," she snapped at him. "You don't get to meet him on your schedule. I thought I made that clear."

"And this is what you want for him?" Pascal waved a hand at the fields, the clouds. "A pretty view? A limitless sky, but no real options? What can he do here besides farm the land or work as staff in the abbey?"

"As he's *five*, we have yet to engage in any hard-hitting conversations about his employment prospects." Her voice was cool. And insulting. "He's more into trucks."

He considered her, and his near-overwhelming urge to get his hands on her. And not because he was angry. That was only a small part of it.

"Thank you," he said in a low voice. "That is the first bit of information about *my son* that you have bothered to give me. Trucks."

She had the grace to flinch at that. And then look away. "People live perfectly happy lives here, as hard as that appears to be for you to understand."

"Maybe so. But why would you deny him the world on the off chance that he will be one of those people?"

"I understand that the simple life doesn't appeal to you," she threw at him, the cold wind tossing her hair about her. She shoved it back and held it off her forehead as she glared at him. "But that speaks more to your snobbery than any lack in it."

Pascal studied her, as she stood there, hair in a mess and clearly cold, with her body between him and her cottage.

As if she could fend him off if he wanted to walk in that door and handle this his way. Right now.

The urge to do exactly that was like a physical pain inside him.

He had dreamed of his little boy's face. He had imagined it.

He supposed this was *longing*, this rough-edged ache that pulsed in him and left him feeling empty.

Behind her the cottage looked warm and cozy. He could see the buttery light from within, and even though it was winter, he could see the remains of summer flowers and the planting that must take place in spring. As if this was a house well loved. It *looked* happy.

Pascal couldn't bear to think about how easily he could have gone home after his date in Rome, slept, then resumed his life. He might never have come here again. He might never have known.

And he didn't know what to call the thing that moved in him then, all teeth and claws and *what-ifs*.

Cecilia stood there before him, her cheeks flushed from the chill and her arms folded across her chest as if to ward off the plummeting temperatures. As if he was the enemy when she was the one who had done this. She was the one who had hidden away here with this secret she'd had no intention of sharing with him.

"I told you I was staying here," he growled at her. "Did you think I would change my mind?"

"Maybe I hoped you would," she replied.

With a bitter flash of honesty that he could have done without.

It was not until he had taken his leave of her—to stomp his spleen into the frozen fields as he tramped around the valley—that he understood why he couldn't quite bring himself to view her as evil. The way he thought he should. On the contrary, something about the way she'd stood up to him—bodily—made his chest ache, and it wasn't until he was back in his stark, monastic chamber that he understood why.

He would have given anything, or everything if asked, to see his mother stand up for him. Even once.

But Marissa Del Guardia had stood for nothing. Not for herself, and certainly not for the child she'd never wanted who had ruined her happiness—something she had no qualm telling him directly. His father had swept in and swept her off her feet as if she was a flower to pick from a garden instead of a waitress in a restaurant he frequented. He'd used her as he liked, then discarded her when she'd fallen pregnant. He had never looked back.

And Marissa's response had been desolation, followed by sleeping pills, and whatever she could find to take the edge off during the day.

Pascal couldn't imagine any circumstance in which she would ever have stirred herself to defend him. He was only surprised she'd actually carried him to term.

He couldn't deny that there was a part of him that liked the fact that his child's mother was prepared to fight off any adversary. Even if that adversary was him.

But by the time a week had dragged by with him marooned in an empty room with only his memories for company and work to dull that noise, Pascal was beginning to lose his famous cool.

It had been educational, to say the least, to discover how much of his business he could handle from afar. It suggested that it wouldn't do him any harm to relax his grip as he had not done since he started. He would need to consider what that meant.

But there was only so much "rusticating" a man could take in the presence of nuns who treated him like an naughty boy, the long shadow of what he'd done here and how he'd left, and the woman who appeared to think she could wait him out and, in effect, steal his child from him all over again.

Pascal wasn't here to address his workaholic tendencies. He was here for his son.

And he'd been ignored as long as he was prepared to take.

So it was almost lowering, really, when he stormed from his room out into the clinic's lobby to find Cecilia waiting for him.

She stood wrapped in a long, camel-colored coat that made her hair gleam and her violet eyes seem fairly purple. She stared at him for a long, solemn moment as if working up to what she meant to say.

"I've been here a week," Pascal pointed out, caring not at all if every person in the clinic beyond was watching and could hear him. "I have sat in my cell and performed my penance. What more can you possibly want from me?"

"That's a dangerous question."

"Shall I beg?" he asked, his voice soft with the menace building in him. They were alone in the foyer for the moment, though he wouldn't have cared if the entire order was lined up around them, singing hymns of praise. "Plead? Or perhaps I should argue my case with a kiss, which seems to be the only time you forget to view me as your enemy? Tell me, which will work? *I want to see my son.*"

He could see her pulse in the hollow of her elegant neck, but it didn't appease him. He didn't care if she was in the grip of the same emotions that buffeted him.

"No such displays are necessary," she said, and this time, he did not attribute the sudden flush in her cheeks to the cold air outside. "I will let you see him."

"You are too kind, Cecilia. Truly."

"That snide tone of voice won't do you any favors," she retorted, her eyes flashing. "I don't have to let you see him at all. And don't get your hopes up. I'm not introducing you to him. Not yet. But as you say, you've been here a week. I expected you to be gone before morning, again. Instead, you stayed and you didn't try to force your way into my cottage."

"I didn't realize I was expected to pass tests," Pascal said icily. "Secret examinations to discover whether or not I'm a decent human being, it appears. I was unaware that was a subject for debate."

"The woman who cares for him while I clean has them running around outside this morning, as it's clear," she said as if he hadn't spoken. But he knew she'd heard him just fine. "You can see him. And before you complain that it isn't enough, you should be aware that my first instinct was to give you nothing at all."

Pascal wasn't sure he could trust himself to speak then, so he said nothing. He merely inclined his head toward the door, and watched as Cecilia wheeled around, then strode out. She looked stiff, her movements jerky—as if her very bones were protesting this.

It only made the dark thing in him solidify.

She kept treating him like he was that wounded soldier who could have died here, forgotten entirely. And he'd let her this whole week because that wounded soldier still lived in him. And because he'd forgotten that, and remembering it again felt like guilt.

But he wasn't the one who had concealed a child for years. Then refused to let her see him.

He followed behind her, thrusting his hands deep into the pockets of his coat as she led him away from the abbey. He could feel her agitation kicking up all around her, so he stayed quiet. She was walking fast and almost ferociously as if she didn't really want to do this. As if she was forcing herself. As if she was afraid that if she slowed down, she wouldn't go through with it.

Pascal didn't really care how this happened, as long as it did.

When they came to the edge of the field on the far side of Cecilia's cottage, she stopped abruptly. There were three children out there, running in circles around a woman. They looked drunk, he thought. As heedless as puppies.

"He's there," Cecilia said, and nodded toward the group. "The one in the middle."

And Pascal stood, stricken, as the two lighter-haired children seemed to fade there before him. Because all he could see was the dark-haired laughing boy between them. He didn't notice his mother or the strange man watching them. He was too busy making circles and shouting out his joy and delight into the cold air.

But Pascal would have recognized him even without Cecilia. Because it was like looking into his own past. It was one of the few photographs he'd ever seen of himself as a child, brought to bright and happy life right there before his eyes.

It took his breath away.

He felt empty and full, and mad with it. Something slammed into him so hard he expected the mountains had come down around them, but nothing moved except the painful kick of his heart against his ribs.

My son.

Dante was sturdy. He ran fast, and joyfully.

He was like a bright light shining there on an otherwise barren field.

He was like a punch, deep into Pascal's gut.

And for a moment Pascal just wanted…everything.

He'd spent a week here, fighting the seduction of this place. This happy, ethereal valley. The peace of it. The ease.

But he couldn't fight the boy in front of him or the woman at his side.

And in an instant it was as if he could suddenly imagine the life he'd left behind when he'd left this place. Her pretty face the first thing he saw in the morning, if he'd stayed. The child they would have raised together. The odd jobs he might have taken, to keep them afloat here. Nothing like the life he had now. He could see it in a long, beautiful sweep of something like memory when it had never happened and couldn't now, and it didn't matter. He wanted it.

God, how he wanted it.

His woman and his little boy and happy, dizzy loops on a cold field.

All the riches in the world, all the power, the revenge on his own father—for a single, piercing moment all of that fell away.

And Pascal had the unsettling notion that he'd sidestepped into a different version of himself, where that fantasy was real. Where he'd never left.

Later he would come up with reasons and rationales. Right here, right now, all he wanted was as much of that everything as he could get, whatever it took.

"Cecilia," he said, turning to look down at her, aware that there must have been some great emotion on his face. He did nothing to hide it. "You must marry me."

CHAPTER SIX

"He wants to marry me," Cecilia said.

It shocked her how hard it was to get the words out of her mouth. Possibly because saying them out loud gave them weight. It made them real. Particularly here, in the kitchen of the abbey where she had eaten so many meals in her time. And now cleaned it as if it was still her own.

Maybe some part of her thought it was.

Mother Superior sat at the long, communal table fashioned of weathered wood where the sisters gathered, her hands cupped around a steaming-hot mug of tea. Cecilia remembered when her hands had been tough, but smoother. Now they were gnarled with the arthritis she never complained about, and something about looking at those familiar, aged hands with those dangerous words floating in the air between them made Cecilia's chest ache.

"Does this surprise you?" Mother Superior asked. Mildly enough.

But then that serene, decidedly calm tone of voice

of hers was one of her superpowers. It made grown men quail before her. It made novitiates tremble. It had made Cecilia cry, more than once.

Today she scowled into the sink she was scrubbing down, and absolutely did not feel the slightest prickle of unwanted moisture behind her eyes.

"Yes. It astonishes me, in fact." She shook her head as if she could shake away all the competing, complicated feelings that had been clattering around inside her since that moment outside on the field when he'd looked at her with that unsettling, raw expression on his face. Then had said what he'd said. "If I'm honest, I think it offends me."

But that wasn't the right word, either. It had felt like a sucker punch, directly into her gut. She'd been faintly amazed that she hadn't doubled over.

A huge, wild ache had ripped opened wide inside her, a crevice so deep and so wide that she'd been terrified for a moment that she might actually topple off the side of the world and disappear inside it. Her heart had pounded so hard, even high in her throat, she'd been terrified she might get sick.

Instead, she'd turned on her heel and walked away from him on legs gone wobbly, not sure she wouldn't simply crumple into the cold ground. But she had to get away from Pascal. At once. Because she thought that if she didn't, she might pull down the mountains all around them with the force of her reaction.

He'd followed, of course.

And there had been too much noise in her head for her to process the things he'd said. The reasons he'd laid down before her like proof. Or some kind of cold, cut-and-dry temptation that was supposed to speak to her somehow when there was that *ache*.

"I'm not dignifying that with a response," she'd said. When she could manage to speak at all.

"There can be only one response," he'd replied. She whipped her head around to stare at him, perhaps imagining that she could shame him out there in the fields she knew too well. The wind had cut into her like knives, but his presence was a far deeper wound by far. How could he imagine otherwise? "I will wait for it, Cecilia."

She was well aware that this time, his *waiting* was a threat. That had been two days ago.

"Why should you be offended?" Mother Superior asked in her maddeningly unbothered way that Cecilia knew full well was *meant* to set her teeth on edge. "What we know about Pascal is that he likes to solve his problems in the most direct way possible. We know what happened when he felt lonely here. Dante is the result."

And it was a measure of how agitated Cecilia was about other things that she forgot to react with her usual mix of emotions at that oblique reference to that morning she had woken up to discover Mother Superior at the foot of a bed she shouldn't have been sleeping in and her whole life changed.

"We know what happened when he left here, and launched himself at the world," Mother Superior continued placidly. "And I'm not the least surprised that his return, wherein he learned that he had a son, should lead to this. It solves all of his problems, elegantly."

"I don't wish to be his problem," Cecilia bit out, her eyes on the sink. "Or have anything to do with solving it for him."

Mother Superior laughed that raspy, lusty laugh of hers that served to remind anyone who heard it that she was, in fact, a woman made of flesh and blood like anyone else. No matter how holy she seemed the rest of the time.

"Child, you have been a problem for that man since the moment he woke up after his accident and saw you there at his bedside," she told Cecilia. "Left to his own devices, he would have taken you with him when he left the first time."

It took a moment for the full meaning of those words to penetrate. When they did, Cecilia set down her sponge, carefully. Very, very carefully. Then she took her time turning and wiping her hands on the apron she wore wrapped around her waist. She was not surprised to find Mother Superior's wise, kind gaze level on hers.

Waiting, she could see. But without a shred of trepidation or concern.

"What do you mean by that?" she asked, though

her voice shook, and worse, she already thought she knew. Hadn't Pascal himself hinted at this in the church? "What do you mean, *left to his own devices*?"

"You did not join us for Morning Prayer," Mother Superior told her, her calm tone scraping down the length of Cecilia's spine like fingernails. "When I went looking for you, I found you in his room. You were still asleep, but he was not."

"Are you… You're not saying…?"

"I merely asked him what his intentions were," Mother Superior replied, that mild gaze not only steady on hers, but distressingly compassionate. "He was a man recovering from an accident who had clearly become well again. I suspected that meant he would not wish to stay with us, tucked away as we are from the rest of the world. Meanwhile, he'd taken it upon himself to despoil a novitiate. I merely wondered what his plans were."

"His plans," Cecilia repeated as if she couldn't comprehend what the other woman was saying. When she did. Too well. "You asked him *his plans.*"

"I merely wondered if he intended to take you with him when he returned to his life, as I had no doubt at all he would do, because that is what men like him are put on this earth to do."

"That was never something we discussed."

But she didn't know if she was saying that to protect him or herself, because while it was true, it was also true that there had been an understanding between them. Or she never would have participated in her *despoiling*, a word she might have found entertaining in other circumstances. When, for example, her *despoiler* was in distant cities the way he was supposed to be instead of holed up in the abbey clinic *right this moment*.

Cecilia wasn't finding any of this entertaining at all.

And Mother Superior was watching her face as if she could read all of this right there on Cecilia's cheeks. That she likely could only made it worse. "What I know about you, child, is that you are not a casual woman," Mother Superior said. "You never have been. You do not give yourself to anything unless you plan to do so with your whole heart and soul for the remainder of your days. It is what would have made you such an excellent nun, if that had been your path. And it is what makes you such a marvelous mother."

And how was she supposed to summon up any self-righteous indignation now? When she said something like that? This was why Mother Superior terrified everyone who came into contact with her—and they thanked her for it.

"I can't… I mean I don't believe…" Cecilia put her hands to her face then, to cover up all the reading material she was broadcasting around the abbey kitchen. And she couldn't tell if she was trembling, or her hands were trembling, or if the earth beneath her feet was rocking and rolling. "Why did you never tell me this?"

"What would have been the point?" Mother Superior asked as if she was genuinely curious. "He left."

"Yes, but…"

And that ache in her was too big. Too vast. She felt as if she was nothing but earthquakes and after-shocks, and beneath it all, there was only the ash and ruin of her first love. Heartbreak masquerading as anger when what she wanted to feel for Pascal and their past was nothing. Not regret, not fury—nothing at all.

How had she managed to convince herself that she could be indifferent to any part of this, much less Pascal himself?

"Do you want me to tell you that he wavered?" Mother Superior asked when the silence only stretched out between them. "Because he did. He argued, and he was torn. But in the end, he left. And yes, I chose to protect you from that. What difference would it make to you that it was difficult for him?"

"I don't know. But it would have, surely."

Because it made a difference now. It seemed to coil inside her, warming her. And the warmth made her feel steadier. It helped her breathe.

"Would it?" Mother Superior smiled faintly. "First you thought you would rededicate yourself to your faith. And then it turned out you were pregnant, and you had to wrestle with whether or not to keep the baby or give it over to adoption. Would his wavering have helped you learn how to be strong enough to grapple with these decisions?"

"I'm not sure it was your call to make." Cecilia's voice was harsher than she'd intended, and it made her stomach hurt. Because she had never spoken to Mother Superior before like that. Never.

She rather expected the ancient abbey to come tumbling down all around them at her impertinence, but it remained solid. The walls did not so much as shiver in response.

Worse, Mother Superior only smiled a little more deeply.

"I'm not sure it was, either," she replied, which made all the emotion inside Cecilia feel heavier. Thicker. Because it was hard to focus on blame and fury when the other woman wasn't defending herself. "That is my weight to carry. What you must decide is what you plan to do about it now."

Cecilia turned back to the sink, blinking back the obnoxious sting of moisture in her eyes that she told herself was blame and fury in spades, no matter how heavy it felt. It was still a betrayal, and from the least likely source imaginable. It was far too much *emotion*, with nowhere to go. No outlet at all.

Only the seismic shifts inside her.

"I plan to do exactly what I've been doing," she said, and she was proud that her voice didn't shake. And that she wasn't gritting out her words through her teeth. "My life may not be what I planned it to be when I was twenty, but that's not necessarily a bad thing. It's full. I'm proud of it. I don't need him."

"And your son?"

"Dante *certainly* doesn't need him." And she found that she was gritting her teeth after all.

"Does he not?" Mother Superior made a clicking noise with her tongue. "It was my impression that children bloomed in the presence of both their parents, should they have that as an option."

"I had neither parent," Cecilia shot back at her. Or to the bottom of the sink anyway. "And I'm perfectly fine."

"You had an entire abbey, child. You still do."

"And so does Dante."

"Cecilia," Mother Superior said in that particularly gentle way of hers that was nothing but iron beneath. "There's a difference between accepting a circumstance, even thriving in it, when you have no other choice. You have done so admirably. You always have. But Dante has choices you did not. Will you let your personal feelings about his father dictate those choices?"

Cecilia's eyes were blurry now, and she didn't turn back around because she didn't want Mother Superior to see it. Though she suspected the old woman could see straight through her, either way.

"You say that as if I don't know what's best for Dante. As if I don't want what's best for him."

"I know you love that child," Mother Superior said soothingly. "And you have worked so hard to give him what you think you lacked. But Cecilia. I don't think it's ever occurred to you that when your mother left you here, she made certain you would be tended to by an entire order of surrogate mothers."

"Of course that's occurred to me. It's why I wanted to join the order myself."

It was also why she had stayed here even in the darkest hours of her disgrace instead of leaving the valley behind. How could she leave the only family she'd ever known? No matter how disappointed they were in her?

"But she also made certain you would never know the faintest bit of information about your own father," Mother Superior continued. "I flatter myself that the sisters and I have done our best, but we can only be surrogate mothers, aunts and sisters. You may not recall that when you were about seven, all you wanted was a father. And you cried and cried for what could never be."

She'd forgotten that. But she shook her head. "It was a phase. It faded."

"Child. Why would you choose to do to Dante what was forced upon you? Would you not spare him that pain if you could?"

And that was the question that stuck with Cecilia as she finished up her duties in the abbey that day, then took the longer walk home so as to make sure she didn't stray too close to the clinic. It was the question that echoed around inside her when she picked Dante up from her neighbor and gazed down at him with the usual mix of fondness and exasperation as he shouted the events of his day at her. Rapid and loud, the way he always did when he was overexcited—and he was usually overexcited.

She thought about the question all throughout their normal afternoon and evening. She considered it during bath time, when Dante leaped out of the tub and ran in circles around the cottage, laughing maniacally and waving his hands over his head until Cecilia could do nothing but laugh with him.

She read him a story, heard his prayers and tucked him into bed, and when she turned out the light and left him to sleep, she could still hear Mother Superior's calm, measured voice inside her.

She'd forgotten—or she'd tried to forget—how much and how often she'd imagined herself with a real family when she'd been young. Cecilia had loved growing up in the abbey. All the sisters had treated her as their own, a very junior sister or everyone's child, and she had never doubted that she was loved. And by many.

But she wasn't like the other children in the village. All the intricacies of family dynamics were lost on her. And as Mother Superior had said today, she had found it especially trying when she was a little bit older than Dante and entirely too consumed with making sure that she was *normal*. It had been clear to her that she was not, and it had bothered her. How had she forgotten that?

She supposed she'd set so much of it aside when she decided to join the order herself that she'd somehow managed to wipe it all out in her memory.

Or perhaps you wanted to join the order because it tied up the story of your life in a nice, neat bow, a voice inside her suggested archly.

She scowled at herself as she cleaned up the kitchen. Then she went to sit out in the main room of the cottage. It was a pleasant, open space that felt airy and large when it was neither. She curled up in her favorite chair before the fire, where she liked to read or sew, and did neither tonight. Instead, she stared into the flames, able to see nothing at all but Mother Superior's deft, dear hands wrapped around her tea. And that voice of hers, so gentle and so soft, that sat in her like a stone.

Why would you choose to do to Dante what was forced upon you?

Cecilia blew out a long, hard breath, and then made herself get up again. She crossed back to the kitchen drawer where she'd thrown the bit of paper she'd found thrust beneath her door one morning. It was a mobile number written in a bold, impatient hand and an initial. *P.*

And maybe it was telling that she hadn't tossed it straight into the fire, but she hadn't.

She stared down at the number and that *P* for a long time.

And when she couldn't put it off any longer, she decided she couldn't face a telephone call. She picked up her mobile and texted him instead. Simple and to the point.

This is Cecilia. We need to talk. Can you come to the cottage?

She told herself he would likely take his time replying, but his response came within seconds.

On my way.

And then Cecilia was treated to some more hard truths about herself, because she…dithered.

There was no other word for it. Before she'd texted him, she hadn't given a thought to her appearance, here at the end of a long day cleaning ancient buildings and tending to an active five-year-old. Or her clothes. The moment he replied, she rushed into her bedroom and found herself changing from her usual loose shirt and comfortable lounging pants into a wholly uncharacteristic shift dress she usually wore only to church. And then smoothing her hair and coiling it into a tidy knot at the nape of her neck.

Then she charged back out into the main room and threw herself into a whirlwind tidying session that had her breathing a little too heavily by the time she'd made the place look less like a child's gymnasium and more like an adult's serene living room. Or as close to such a thing as she could get as she was not a billionaire with staff.

That thought kicked her temper back into gear, and she frowned at herself in the reflection of the windows, because why was she trying to *impress* Pascal? Surely she should have gone the other direction and left herself and the cottage as slovenly as possible, the better to drive him away.

But she didn't change her clothes again.

Nor did she empty the basket of Dante's favorite toys across the rug, the better to be crunched painfully underfoot.

And at some point she would have to face what it meant that she wanted so desperately for Pascal to see her, and this home she'd made for their child, at their best. Just as she would have to face the electric charge within her at the notion he was coming here, and her sneaking suspicion that it was not agitation that was so bright inside her.

She was terribly afraid it was pure, undiluted anticipation.

Another betrayal in a day chock full of them.

When his knock came on her front door—a hard, commanding rap—her stomach fluttered about as if it was beset by butterflies and she hated herself. Fully. But she crossed the floor to let him in anyway.

She wrenched open the door, prepared to be icily controlled and cuttingly polite, and caught her breath.

Because she was never prepared.

Pascal stood there, in profile as he stared off toward the lit-up abbey in the darkness. The light from inside the cottage spilled over him, making a meal out of his strong nose and sensual lips. Even his scars seemed to enhance his appeal, silvery across his jaw, then disappearing beneath the collar of the coat he wore.

He took his time turning his head to look at her, and when his eyes met hers, the world began to burn.

Her first and foremost.

"I have raced to your side on command," he said, his voice low and laced with too many dark things she did not wish to understand. Not when she could feel them all, each individual thread and threat, winding around and around inside her. "Never let it be said that I cannot take an order, *cara*. Like a dog."

Cecilia ignored the way that wound its way down her spine, settling worryingly low in her belly with a pulse she wanted to call pain. But it wasn't pain.

It most certainly wasn't pain.

She forced herself to turn her back on him, then led him into the room as if he was as threatening to her as the tottery old priest—even when every alarm inside her shouted that it was exactly the wrong thing to do. That she should never turn her back on a predator like him, no matter how many too-hot memories she had of a time she'd been pretending she'd forgotten.

But she did it, and though her neck prickled, Pascal did not leap upon her with his fangs bared, or any such superstitious nonsense. *Of course he didn't*, she told herself sternly. She waved him to the sofa before the fire, with its newly plumped pillows and a throw folded just so along the back to hide the stains from small, sticky hands. Then she took her favorite chair again, stuck as it was at a convenient angle to the sofa that allowed her to be close yet not in reach.

"No offer of a drink?" he asked as he shrugged out of his heavy coat and tossed it beside him on the sofa. And then he sat, managing to overwhelm the small sofa with the sheer magnitude of his oversize frame and those *shoulders*. Cecilia somehow doubted she would ever look at that sofa quite the same way again. "No *aperitivos* to help us pretend we're civilized?"

"This isn't a social call."

"Not even a few olives. I feel like a savage."

"That is between you and whatever passes for your god, Pascal," she said tightly.

She regretted it the moment she spoke. And then with far more fervor when his stark mouth moved into something far too sharp to be a smile.

"Incivility does not suit you, Cecilia."

"I brought you over here to discuss introducing you to Dante," she said, reminding herself that she needed to stay cool, controlled. No matter how his presence here seemed to suck up all the air in the main room, making it nearly impossible to breathe. "But the more you play little games, the more I second-guess myself on that score."

The hint of amusement on his face was extinguished as surely as if it had never been there, and she detested the fact that she could *feel* it. As if he was doing it *to* her. And that terrible pang of something like panic, urging her to do whatever she could to make it come back.

No, she ordered herself. *This is not about placating him. This is about choosing between right and wrong.*

But he was looking at her as if she was the enemy. "I suggest that you proceed with caution. Do you truly wish to set up a scenario in which we use our child as a bargaining chip between us?"

Cecilia blinked. "That's not what I meant."

"I can't pretend to know what you have been thinking about while you made me sit in that clinic and relive the worst time of my life," he said in the same dark tone, his gaze so hard on hers that she was surprised her skin didn't open beneath the onslaught. "Revenge, I assume. But in between amusing memories of my accident and what it took to survive it, I have been entertaining myself with tales from the worst divorces."

Once again she hadn't seen him coming. A sensation she did not enjoy. "Divorces? What do divorces have to do with our situation?" She tilted her head to one side. "Or is that what passes for your usual leisure reading material?"

"I was studying custody battles," he supplied, and he settled back against the couch. Another man might have looked idle. Pascal did not. "The nastier, the better. And do you know who suffers the most in such scenarios? Not the battling parents."

It was the second time today that someone else had obliquely rebuked her for her selfishness, and Cecilia found it didn't sit well. She was far too flushed. And she wanted to throw the lamp beside her at his head for daring to lecture *her* on parenting, even in a roundabout way.

But she had spent most of her life learning discipline of one sort or another, so she kept herself still.

"You don't think we should use Dante as a bargaining chip, and I agree, of course," she said when she could be certain the lamp would remain where it was. "Perhaps you could also stop trying to use him to manipulate my emotions."

She expected him to argue. Instead, something in his black eyes gleamed gold. He lifted one finger as if to shrug without bothering to expend the energy required. Somehow that small gesture was breathtakingly infuriating.

"Fair enough," he said. Which was even more irritating. Cecilia hadn't expected him to be remotely agreeable—and in fact, she went still when he smiled at her, because she knew better. "But I know about him now. There's no going back from that, no matter how much of a grace period I give you to deal with the reality you already knew. Surely you must understand this."

He was giving *her* a grace period—Cecilia ordered herself to breathe before she exploded. Especially because there was something about the way he gazed at her that made her think an explosion was precisely what he wanted.

"I would prefer not to be threatened by you at every opportunity," she managed to retort. She laced her fingers together in her lap when all he did was raise that dark brow of his, because throwing lamps would not solve the problem. No matter how satisfying it might be in the moment. "I cannot deny Dante access to his father. Just because he hasn't asked about you before now doesn't mean he won't in the future. I suppose I've been in denial about that."

He only watched her, and though he still lounged there on the sofa, she didn't make the mistake of imagining that he was at ease. His entire body was poised. Alert. As if he might spring into action at the slightest provocation. She didn't want to speculate what kind of action that might be.

Cecilia swallowed and found her throat dry. And forced herself to keep going, even though it was hard, because this was ultimately about Dante. And there was nothing she wouldn't do for him. Even this.

"I don't have a father," she said matter-of-factly. "There's no possibility of my figuring out who he was, and at this point in my life, I'm not sure I would want to even if I could." She held his gaze, though it made her skin feel much too tight. "And I know your experience with your father was no easier."

He didn't laugh, though his dark eyes gleamed. "That is putting it more politely than he deserves."

She inclined her head and extended her olive branch. "I don't see any reason why Dante should have to suffer the things that we did, if we can prevent it."

"This is very noble-minded of you, Cecilia, after all these years that handily belie that sentiment," Pascal said, and his tone was so sardonic it seemed to lodge itself between her ribs like a bullet. "How exactly do you imagine this high-minded approach to our child's life will unfold, practically speaking?"

That was certainly not the expression of gratitude she'd anticipated. Cecilia sat a little bit straighter in her chair, and frowned at him. "What do you mean?"

"I assume you will oversee the initial introduction, as it were." Another flick of that finger, a shrug and a dismissal in one. She wanted to slap at it. "That makes sense. Perhaps you should take this opportunity to outline your ideal visitation schedule."

She felt herself go still as if she'd blundered into a trap in the woods and had only just noticed the steel jaws lying there, primed to slam closed. "If everything goes well, you can come and visit him whenever you like."

"Very generous indeed." His dark eyes glittered. "But you see, I do not understand why you should get to control how much I see the child that you've concealed from me all this time. Perhaps he should come and live with me, and you can come visit him whenever you like." He smiled then, and it was not a pleasant smile. It was all steel and jagged edges. "Behold my generosity."

"I'm his mother!" she snapped at him, not sure if it was fury or fear racing through her then. Both, perhaps. She caught herself. "A child needs his mother."

"A child needs his father, *cara*. Particularly a boy. Everyone knows this."

"Are you threatening to take him away from me?" she asked, throwing it out there because it was the worst thing. And it was better to keep it right there in the light, where she could see it.

Not that seeing *him* in the cheery light of this cottage that had always seemed so safe and happy to her before tonight was doing her any favors.

"I do not make threats." Pascal was still lounging, one arm tossed down the length of the couch's back, his long legs thrust out before him. But his gaze was dark and intense and focused entirely on her. "You have vastly underestimated the seriousness of the situation, I think."

"Of the two people sitting in this room, I'm the one who's been raising a child alone. I don't think it's possible to underestimate that situation."

"I mean me." And she realized for the first time that he wasn't sitting like that because he was pretending to be at ease. He was doing it to keep himself in check. He was doing it to keep his hands to himself, and not on any lamps. Or her. Cecilia felt a terrible chill sweep over her. "You have underestimated *me*, Cecilia."

It occurred to her then, as he looked at her with that same lethal steel she could hear in his voice and see all over his powerful body, that she really didn't know this man at all. The Pascal she remembered had been compelling, magnetic and charming. But the kind of power that emanated from the Pascal sitting before her tonight had been little more than a spark in that man. The Pascal sitting before her had created an empire in his name. He had taken what little he had and made it a force to be reckoned with on the global scale.

She had known a grateful patient in a hospital, alone and conversant with his own near-death experience and the relief that he'd survived it.

This man was fully alive in every sense of the term.

And he'd made himself a king.

Had she ever been in control of this situation? But even as the question flashed through her, he was speaking again.

"I allowed the shock to get to me," he said in that same dark, deliberate way that was far more terrifying than any display of temper or emotion. "I spent the first few days here in some kind of a daze, trying to make sense of this thing. But your refusal to engage with me was actually a favor. I should thank you."

"I was protecting my son."

There was a hint of a curve on that stark mouth of his, but no more, and she thought it was cynical, at best. Not anything like a smile.

"You can call it what you like. Once I saw the child, so similar to me in every way, everything crystallized."

He actually shrugged then, with his shoulders. That, too, was worse.

"I don't know what you mean by crystallized," she said, aware that she was talking too quickly. Too nervously. "But I do know that I'm not going to—"

"I've heard a great deal about what you will and will not do, Cecilia," Pascal said, a dark storm in him that she could feel all too well even without any rain. "But now it is time for me to tell you what *I* will and will not do."

"Pascal—"

But it was too late.

His expression was raw again, but this time with a fury that scared her all the more because it was controlled.

"I will not relinquish my claim to my child," he told her. "I will not meekly hand over custody of him. You have already stolen six years of his life from me. I can never get it back."

Another shiver sank down her spine, edged with foreboding. She tried to say his name again, but this time nothing came out.

Too late, something inside her warned.

And she had never seen his black gaze as dark as it was then.

"I don't see any particular reason why I shouldn't take him for the next six years, Cecilia," he said, far too calmly. "Just to make it fair."

CHAPTER SEVEN

PASCAL SHOULD PROBABLY not have taken quite so much satisfaction in seeing her pale.

But then, he had never pretended to be a good man. Save the months he'd spent here, that was, when he hadn't known if he would live through it—and even then, only until the end of it. When he proved himself as lost to decency as ever.

"That is never going to happen," Cecilia threw at him through bloodless lips.

Her hands were in fists in her lap, and she was curled toward him as if she imagined she might take a swing at him.

He almost wished she would.

"It will happen if I want it to happen," he told her, pitiless and very, very certain. "I'm a very wealthy man, *cara*. And wealth is power whether you like it or not, even up here in this valley time has forgotten. Do you really think you could best me in court if I did not allow it?"

"Now we're going to court?" Her voice was fainter then, her color even more pale.

And he almost felt sorry for her; he really did. But he had been here too long, with nothing to do but think through all the possibilities—and he'd concluded there was really only one. Only one possible ending to this situation that gave everyone involved what they wanted. Him more than her, perhaps, but then, he hadn't concealed a child from her.

Cecilia hadn't reached the same conclusion yet. But Pascal couldn't say he disliked the opportunity to teach her a lesson as she made her way toward the only possible outcome.

Especially because she still haunted him. Even when he knew what she'd done. Even when she refused to let him meet his own son. None of that seemed to matter when he dreamed of her soft mouth, her honey-colored hair. Those eyes of violet that should not have been possible, and yet were perfectly natural.

She haunted him even now, when she was in the same room, dressed like the date he'd wished he'd had while spending all of that energy looking for an appropriate wife. She didn't look like a cleaner tonight. She was dressed with a simple elegance that made him want to press his mouth to her collarbone, then bury himself inside her, the only way he could take part in that kind of sophisticated poetry.

It had occurred to him at some point over the past

few days that he had been unable to find the perfect wife when he'd looked because he'd already met her. He'd asked her to marry him and she'd refused him, but that was just as well, because it had given him time to understand that his reaction to seeing Dante on that field was just that. A reaction.

He had waited. And he had vowed, with every passing day, that she would marry him as he wished. And she would pay.

Over and over again, until he was satisfied.

And Pascal was rarely satisfied.

"I will do anything and everything I have to do," he told her now, with a quiet intensity he could see rocked her. "If I feel compassionate, I suppose I might allow you to fly down to Rome and see him one weekend a month. Perhaps two."

"One weekend a month—" she began, her voice wild.

But she bit off her own words. And swallowed as if her throat hurt, keeping them all inside. Then she blinked rapidly enough that he suspected it was tears of frustration she was trying to keep at bay.

"I asked you to come over here tonight to discuss Dante's best interests," she said after a long moment of keeping herself together. She'd even managed to keep her voice even. "Which I've come to understand included you taking on the role of his father."

"I am his father. There is no role to take on. It is a fact."

"But you don't seem to have any idea about what might be good for him or you wouldn't suggest these things." Another hard, visible swallow. And Pascal found himself fascinated by the telltale pulse in her neck. It told him how agitated she truly was, no matter how calm she might be pretending to be. "Let me remind you that I'm the woman you made all manner of promises to, all of which you broke when you disappeared. I have no reason to assume you won't do the same thing to my child. And instead of giving me the space to work through this—"

"You had six years, Cecilia."

"—you decided to throw your weight around instead."

And by that point, of course, she was no longer quite so calm. He noted that the color had come back to her cheeks, and her eyes were a violet storm. Her hands were still in fists, though she was still holding them in her lap. She looked well and truly agitated.

Good.

"You have two choices," Pascal told her, his voice implacable. "You can accept the fact that this is out of your hands. You will see the child at my whim, or possibly not at all, as it suits me."

"That's obviously not possible." Her voice shook. "*Of course* that's not possible. What's the other choice?"

"I told you," he said, and he couldn't keep the satisfaction from his voice. Then again, he didn't try very hard. "Marry me. Then you can see him all you like."

She made a soft noise, then shot up from her chair. He had the impression she wanted to launch herself at him, and even braced himself for the impact, but she didn't. Instead, she moved toward the fire, folding her arms across her chest as if she needed to hold herself intact. Pascal stayed where he was, settling back against the couch, and waited for this endgame of his to play itself out.

Or for her to look at him again.

He frowned at his own bizarre sentimentality, but brushed it away when she began to speak—her attention directed at the fire.

"I don't understand why you would wish to marry someone you think so little of," she said, sounding... subdued.

Pascal made a small opera out of a shrug and a sigh to match. "Whatever I might think of you personally, not to mention the questionable choices you've made, you're obviously an excellent mother to my child. He is as you said he was. Healthy, happy."

And if she didn't already know that of course he'd gone and looked at the boy again without her permission, well. Her denial was not his problem. He had kept his distance. And not because he was interested in obeying her dictates—or anyone else's—but because he had no interest in scaring off his own son.

He would wait for his introduction. Then he would do exactly as he pleased.

Cecilia waited as if she expected him to keep talking, then let out a sound that he couldn't quite define when he didn't. "That doesn't explain why you would want to marry me."

He remembered that moment at the side of the field when it had all gotten to him. When he had found himself swamped with a kind of longing he had since dismissed. Because he was Pascal Furlani, not some soft, emotional creature. He had been reacting to the shock, that was all.

It had been a long, long time since anyone had managed to surprise him.

But he had been given a great many days to accustom himself to this new development in his life. He had a son. That was what mattered. And a son deserved a family. So Pascal could marry his son's mother or he could marry someone else—he didn't much care which, but he was going to make Dante a family.

One way or another, he was going to spend his son's first Christmas with a father like the family man his board of directors did not believe he could be.

"I am a deeply unromantic man," he told Cecilia. He waited as she turned slightly so she could look at him again. "My mother spent a great deal of time carrying on about her great love affair. It shadowed the whole of our lives. And as the result of that affair, I can assure you, love had nothing to do with it."

He could see her take that in and consider it.

"So the marriage you're proposing is in name only."

Pascal saw the faint flare of something like hope in her gaze, too.

Maybe that was why he laughed.

Or maybe he was a bastard in more than simple, biological fact.

"I don't need you to be in love with me, if that's what you mean," he said, again enjoying himself more than he should. "And I'm not capable of love myself. I require a wife in any case. I've been searching for one for some time. The trouble was, I did not wish there to be a hint of scandal attached to her."

"I'm the most scandalous woman in this village," Cecilia said. Clearly hoping that would disqualify her from consideration. "I'm obviously not the right choice for a man of your…stature."

That *stature* was not the word she'd meant to use was obvious enough that Pascal almost thought her intended word glimmered in the air between them, like the heat from the fire.

"Your only scandal is me." And when he saw her gaze take on a calculating gleam, he laughed again. "Do not bother to tell me otherwise. According to all sources in and out of the abbey, I was your only mistake. Which makes you perfect for my purposes."

"I feel certain that I want nothing to do with what you call perfection."

"You have a choice, *cara*," he said, drawling a little as he said it. "Never let it be said I am not magnanimous."

She looked like she wanted to strangle him, which should probably not have made him hard in instant, enthusiastic response.

"Yes," she seethed at him. "*Magnanimous* is precisely the word I would have chosen to describe you."

"Should you choose to marry me, you will be doing me a favor," Pascal continued, almost happily. "You will help me to create a charming picture of domesticity to undercut my board of directors' machinations. You've already met a pair of them. They are always scheming against me, and the fact that I'm a single, seemingly unfettered man does not endear me to them. I can't say that I will ever forgive what you have done here, but my gratitude will be no small thing, I trust."

He could have told her that he also wanted Dante to have the family he'd never had. But he didn't.

"Your gratitude," she repeated, her voice flat. "Or, excuse me, your *potential* gratitude is what I am to look forward to."

"Or you can look forward to a weekend a month. Supervised, of course. Noncustodial parents do have a reputation for disappearing with their children, don't they?"

"And what if I don't believe you?" she asked after another long moment. He could see she was fighting to keep her composure. "What if I think you're just trying to intimidate me?"

"Five-year-olds are resilient," he said with the soft ruthlessness that made even the normally cheeky Guglielmo pause and rethink. "It would be *nice* to have you there when I meet him. It would be *nice* to have you set the stage. But it is not necessary, Cecilia. If I were you, I would not forget that."

"Or what?" she demanded, wildly. "You'll just… steal him away to Rome?"

"Yes." His voice was a hard crack in the quiet room. "Without a second thought."

She stared back at him, stricken. And she was his ghost, once upon a time his angel. But he didn't let that soften him. If anything, that he had believed he cared for her all those years ago made the betrayal worse. He stared back at her, relentless.

"Mama?" The small voice came from one of the doors behind Pascal. "I heard voices."

Pascal tensed. He watched Cecilia's face closely. And he was sure he could see her fight back the urge to shoo the child away. To have him hide himself just a little longer, however futile the gesture.

He thought he saw something like despair in her otherworldly eyes, just a flash of it. Just enough to lodge itself inside Pascal like shame.

But then she smiled. Wide and bright as if there

had never been anything in her eyes but sweetness and light.

"Come here, baby," she said, and held out her hand. "You have a very special visitor tonight."

Pascal held himself still enough to crack in half as he heard Dante's surprisingly heavy footsteps move across the floor. And then he watched as the small, sturdy boy with rosy cheeks and black hair standing on end came around the side of the couch. He walked toward the fire and took his mother's hand. Then he gazed at Pascal with sleepy eyes.

Sleepy eyes that were black like Pascal's, with a dark rim around the irises that Pascal suspected, were he any closer, would be the precise violet shade of his mother's.

It was like a heart attack, but it didn't hurt. It simply…seized Pascal where he sat.

He knew this child. He could see the shape of his own face in the smaller face before him. He could see his own mother's nose. And he could see Cecilia, too. And it had never occurred to Pascal before that children were the real ghosts, patchworks of the past made new—yet unlike the haunts of fiction, wholly uninterested in what had gone before them.

Pascal felt struck down, though he knew he still sat in the same position. He felt everything he'd felt on that field and more, because this time, his son was right in front of him. *Looking* at him.

And Pascal had never understood his father or his

choices. But here, now, in this huge moment that was happening so quietly and calmly despite the cacophony inside him, he understood the man even less.

Because he knew that he would fight, kill, or die for this little boy with his sleepy eyes and sulky mouth. He would not think twice.

That his father had walked away from *his* son made even less sense to Pascal now.

"Dante," Cecilia said, her voice soft but perfectly cheerful as if this had been her plan all along, and Pascal stopped thinking about that useless, spineless man who shared nothing with him but biology. "This is your father."

The little boy stared. He regarded Pascal solemnly. One beat, another.

"Okay," he said.

Then he yawned, wide enough to crack his jaw, didn't spare his mother or brand-new father a second glance, and shuffled his way back to his bed.

They married the following week by special license.

Pascal stood at the very altar where he had first discovered the existence of the child who had changed everything. Dante—his *son*, he reminded himself with that same fierce pride that beat in him now like a new heartbeat—stood beside him, looking proud and overtly solemn in his best clothes.

Dante looked up at him, his little face grave. Pascal didn't think it through. He reached down and put his hand on his child's head, something sweet and unexpected blooming in him at the sensation. At the way the curve of his palm fit the crown of Dante's head.

As if they had been crafted to fit together like this, interlocking pieces. Father and son.

He told himself that was why he felt very nearly emotional when the nuns who filled the pews began to sing, a hauntingly lovely song that he realized belatedly was their version of a wedding march.

Then Cecilia appeared at the head of the small church's aisle, and Pascal…stared.

She was unhappy with him. She had made no secret of it in the days between that night when she had finally accepted reality, and now.

"What concerns me is how Dante will handle this," she had said that night, still stiff and unfriendly at the fireplace after the child had gone back to bed. "You've only just sprung the fact that you're his father on him. I'm not sure how a wedding between me and a stranger is going to strike him."

"Children are resilient," Pascal said with great unconcern.

"You know that, do you?" she blazed at him. "With all your experience handling children? Raising them?"

"If I lack experience raising children, Cecilia," he'd replied silken and dangerous, "whose fault is that?"

And she had paled, but she hadn't backed down. "He's more fragile than he looks."

"If children were not resilient, neither you nor I would be here today. And yet here we are."

She had let out a shaky sort of breath. "I don't know that I think we should base anything on your childhood or mine. In fact, I imagine that the wisest course of action is to think about our childhoods and do the precise opposite."

Cecilia had decided that they should tell Dante that they were marrying together. As the united front she insisted they would have to become if any of this was to work. Pascal did not remind her that she was no longer in control of the terms—or anything else. He assumed that must have been obvious to her already.

"And by work," she snapped at him when he arrived the following morning at the appointed time, "I do not mean to your satisfaction. I mean, we have to find a way to make sure this is about Dante. Because it can only be about Dante."

"Whatever else could it be about, Cecilia?" he had asked. Silkily enough that she'd flushed.

But when Dante was told of their plan, he'd grinned. "Do we get to be a family? Everyone else gets to be a family."

"Yes," Cecilia had said, her voice suspiciously rough and her eyes too bright. "We would get to be a family. We would all live under one roof. But it wouldn't be here. We would have to move down to Rome, where your father lives."

The little boy had seemed far more concerned with the toy truck he was slamming repeatedly into the leg of the sofa then the conversation.

"Paolo's mother told me about Rome," he said matter-of-factly. "She's from there. You can get gelato anytime you want. Not only when the abbey cook makes it."

"And there you have it," Pascal murmured. "Easy."

The look Cecilia had given him then was murderous.

And he was twisted enough to enjoy that, too.

She hadn't objected when Pascal had spent the rest of the intervening days as much with Dante as possible. He walked the boy to his care. And didn't bother to discuss his feelings on the topic of the soon-to-be Signora Furlani spending her days cleaning, because she only had so many days left here. If she wanted to spend them on her hands and knees on unforgiving stone floors, it was nothing to him.

It was on one of those days that she found him in his little cell, tending to the work that was always piling up on his laptop. He heard a faint noise, looked up—and there she was, standing in his doorway with a mop clenched in one hand.

And for a moment it was as if they'd been tossed back in time. He had the oddest notion that if he looked down at himself, he would find all the bandages and wounds he'd had when he'd first come here. As if the accident had only just happened.

As if maybe they could do this over—though he shoved that thought away almost as soon as it formed.

And he knew she was thinking much the same thing from that stricken, electric look in her beautiful violet eyes.

It was those eyes he'd seen first when he'd surfaced after the surgery that had saved his life. Those eyes that had insinuated themselves somehow into the confusion of his brain in those fuzzy days, and had tempted him to make his way back to the land of the living.

And it was those eyes that slammed into him again now, making a mockery of his assertion that he was only here—and only doing this—for the boy.

But he chose not to analyze that.

"Dante is putting on a good show," she told him after a moment, her hand tight around the mop handle. "But sooner or later this is all going to come crashing down on him. I hope you're prepared for it. He's a headstrong, often maddening, perfect little boy. I doubt very much that your life is set up to accommodate an active five-year-old."

"The beauty of my life, *cara*, is that it is set up to accommodate me. Therefore, whatever it is I wish it to be, it becomes."

"Spoken like a man who has no idea what I'm

talking about," she retorted. "And yes," she continued before he could remind her yet again why it was he had no experience in this area, "I know. It's my fault. But you're the one issuing ultimatums, Pascal. Not me."

He knew what she meant was, he was the one who insisted on marrying her, and was holding her child over her head to make sure she did it. Something he supposed he ought to have felt some guilt about. Oddly enough, his conscience was clear.

"The other thing I have, in abundance, is money," Pascal said. And smiled faintly when she rolled her eyes. "I'm not bragging, Cecilia. Do you know what that money buys? Nannies. Tutors. An army of trained staff to make sure his is the best nursery in Italy. Anything and everything that can make this transition as painless as possible for Dante. And for me."

"But not me, of course." She eyed him as he lounged there on the narrow bed, his laptop open before him. Not in a particularly friendly manner. "Are you not concerned with my transition?"

"Not especially."

She ran her tongue over her teeth. "What is it you expect me to do?"

Pascal studied her a moment. "I suppose you could clean my floors if you desired, but my housekeeper would not be best pleased."

Her eyes flashed. "There's no shame in cleaning a floor."

"In general, no," he'd replied. "But we are talking about the wife of Pascal Furlani, not a nameless single mother in a remote mountain village."

And he didn't have the slightest intention of telling her that the way she glared at him made him want to poke at her more, not less.

"There will be certain expectations upon you," he said.

"You mean your expectations."

"Mine, yes, but sadly for you, not only mine." Or he would keep her naked and tied to his bed. He didn't know quite why he didn't say that out loud. But he had to shift to keep that image from making him reveal too much to her. "You have to be outfitted with an appropriate wardrobe, first and foremost. Then I will have to consider the best way to instruct you in how best to move in the society I keep. Appearances, you understand."

"You must be joking." When he only gazed back at her, she scoffed. "It's not as if you're royalty, is it? You're a businessman."

"There are many things I learned the hard way," Pascal said quietly. "If you do not wish to profit from my example, that is all the same to me. You can flail around, making a spectacle of yourself if that is what you wish. I will allow it."

Not that he could actually imagine this woman *flailing* in any capacity.

"Will it embarrass you?" she asked coolly. "Because if so, it holds a certain appeal."

"I can handle the embarrassment," Pascal replied easily. "But can Dante? Children can be so cruel."

And he had allowed himself a smile when she simply stalked off down the hallway, slamming her cleaning tools about with entirely too much force.

Their wedding day could not come soon enough to suit him.

"I thought you would lecture me," he had said to Mother Superior earlier today when he'd seen her after he'd dressed.

"Would that work, do you imagine?" the old woman asked him, that canny gaze of hers on him. "Would you listen?"

"I listened to you last time," he reminded her as they made their way to the church. "Why not again?"

"You listened to your fear, child," she said when they made it to the door. "I was nothing but a catalyst. And I'll thank you to remember, when fear starts whispering in your ear again, that all it made you was alone."

"And very rich," he'd said drily.

"The abbey looks forward to your significant donation," she'd replied tartly.

And Pascal didn't know why he was thinking about an old, interfering nun's pointed remarks at a time like this. When he was standing here in this church and Cecilia was floating toward him like one of those dreams that had chased him through all the years they'd been apart.

She wore a cream-colored gown and a demure veil, but he could still see her.

Once upon a time she had saved him. Then she had betrayed him. Now she would marry him, and he couldn't help thinking that he'd find the balance in it there. In their marriage.

And better still, in the marriage bed.

He had already kissed her far too thoroughly and long in this very same church, and lightning had failed to strike him down. Thoughts of marital congress were hardly likely to bring the walls down around them.

She arrived beside him and he took her hand, and then it was happening.

The priest was quick. The nuns made approving noises.

Pascal said, "I do" loud enough to be heard in that stark white clinic room he never planned to enter again.

Cecilia's vows were more measured, but she said them. She didn't stumble. She didn't pause for effect.

And then it was time for Pascal to lift her veil and smooth it back from her face.

He felt something like rage pound through him, thick and nearly mad, and it took him a moment to realize it wasn't rage at all. It was triumph.

As if this was about her, not the boy.

But he refused to let himself consider that.

He kissed her instead, with all the pent-up passion of the years she had kept his child from him and the days she'd forced him to sit in that clinic as penance. He kissed her deep, and thorough, and he didn't care if he made the watching nuns uncomfortable.

He kissed her until there was no doubt whatsoever that he was claiming what was his.

And when he lifted his head, she looked stunned. Thrown.

That, too, felt like a victory.

Dante ran before them down the aisle toward the door. Pascal took Cecilia's hand and led her after their son, something primitive working its way through him as they moved. His son. His woman.

His family, at last.

"I want you to be very clear about something," his brand-new wife said when they stepped outside into the December morning. It was clear, but very cold.

Cecilia didn't shiver. She kept her gaze on his while Dante ran in a big, looping circle around Pascal's waiting car.

"I am not certain things have ever been more clear, *cara*," he told her. Truthfully.

Her violet eyes met his, then held. She tipped up her chin.

"You forced me to do this," she said, "and I did it. For Dante. But you should know right now that it doesn't matter if you kiss me like that. This marriage will never, ever be consummated."

Pascal laughed.

Then he slid his hand along her pretty face and held her cheek in the palm of his hand. He met that outraged violet glare and he smiled at her, because he knew this part. He knew how to get what he wanted, and he would. It was what he did.

"My darling wife," he said, enjoying the words as much as the way she trembled—in fury, he was sure, and he liked that, too. He couldn't wait to taste it. "You will beg me."

CHAPTER EIGHT

ROME WAS A SPARKLING, sprawling mess of a too-big city, Cecilia was a wife when she had never planned to marry—much less in such haste and upon command—and there wasn't a single part of this sudden new life she was going to have to find her way through, one way or another, that made any sense to her.

Pascal had driven them down from the mountains, stopping only for the odd meal or the chance to stretch his legs. Or better still, to let Dante wear himself out enough to resume the trip. For her part, Cecilia had changed into a traveling outfit after the ceremony, too aware that it was an outfit her brand-new husband—her *husband*—had picked out for her. She hadn't wanted to wear anything he'd given her, but she also didn't want any of the nuns to know how fraught and strained her brand-new marriage was. Already.

"I don't want you to dress me," she'd told him, scowling over the clothes he'd delivered to her the night before the ceremony. A wedding dress, traveling clothes and a sharp order to leave all her packing to the staff he planned to unleash on the cottage after they left. His staff would take all the personal items and leave behind the furniture. Maybe she'd been mad about that, too. Maybe she was mad about everything. "Like some horrid little doll."

"Thus far I have only provided you with the wardrobe I would prefer you to wear," he'd replied in that dark, stirring way of his. His black-gold eyes had glittered. "Would you like me to dress you, as well? Because that is a different proposition altogether."

She didn't want to think about that.

Or to be more precise, it was all she thought about the last long night she was still herself. She'd tossed and turned and scowled at her ceiling, and none of it had changed a thing. She'd woken up, put on the wedding dress he'd chosen for her and walked down the aisle as ordered.

And now she was Pascal's wife.

The truth was, she didn't want to think too hard or too closely about any part of it. Not the wedding ceremony. Not the fact that she'd left behind the only home she had ever known for a future she could only describe as unknown. And unsettled.

And she certainly did not want to think about that taunt of his *after* the ceremony.

She would not beg him. For anything. Ever.

But even as she thought such things, and meant

them, a quick glance toward her new husband—and the way he navigated the roads with confidence and ease—made something deep inside her...quiver.

She busied herself with Dante, who was over-excited and could hardly contain himself over the course of the long drive. There were tears. Tantrums. Too much sugar, not enough videos, and by the time they finally made it all the way into Rome, Pascal was tightlipped and Cecilia was thoroughly frazzled.

But not too frazzled to be a little smug about it.

"Just remember," she told Pascal as they finally got out of the car, there in a garage that was itself almost too fancy for her to take in, "you asked for this."

Pascal only gave her a dark look. Then he picked Dante up—because the boy had finally gone to sleep—and led the way inside. Up a stair and into three full floors of what Pascal called *home*.

Cecilia's first impression had been...overwhelming.

She'd chalked it up to fatigue. All that glittering, all those views, the soaring entry hall that went all the way up to a chandelier the size of her cottage, and all that *stuff* that shrieked its dizzying cost at decibels she didn't think she could truly understand.

The next morning it was even worse.

Because it had been one thing to see magazine spreads of a powerful man in a rich person's clothes. The magazines were filled with such men after all. It was something else again to be steeped in all that power rather than simply reading about it at a remove. To have it wrapped around her, choking her and making her think that she had been very foolish indeed to come here.

All Cecilia had been thinking about when she'd agreed to this was staying close to her child. And that was all that mattered, she told herself sternly that morning as she crept around the huge, hushed apartment that was the largest single residence she'd ever been in. But she should probably also have spared a thought or two for the fact she was a simple woman.

Cecilia's version of a complicated life had included the boundaries of the same small village that was the only home she'd ever known, and the good or bad opinions of the people who lived there with her. And whether she'd lived inside the abbey walls or in a cottage outside the grounds, the abbey that had always been the center of that village had also been her whole world.

You didn't have a choice, she reminded herself tartly. *You had to come here.*

But that didn't make things any better.

She was…dizzy. Whatever the opposite of altitude sickness was. And that feeling didn't go away as the days passed, the darkness of the waning year enlivened only by the signs of Christmas everywhere she looked in her adopted new city.

Pascal had been good to his word. As far as Cecilia could tell, he had employed a literal army of staff to care for Dante's every possible need. Each and every one of whom Dante found fascinating, so as much as Cecilia might have wanted to reclaim her only child's attention, he didn't want to go with her when she sought him out and found him playing, or doing crafts, or practicing scales on the piano that had its own room. He wanted to continue doing what he was doing, in the company of all the new people who he, of course, found far more entertaining and fascinating than his own mother.

"I don't know what you expect me to do with myself now that you've forced me to come here," she had seethed at Pascal one morning several days after they'd arrived, feeling brittle enough that she might break in two. "I am not used to all this idleness."

Pascal had been in the office he used when he was home, starting his day with a stack of financial papers from around the world and a cup of the strong espresso he preferred.

The look he'd given her had seared through her.

"You are in Rome," he'd said, sounding faintly astonished that such a thing needed to be said. Or perhaps that was his innate arrogance. "If you cannot entertain yourself here, Cecilia, you cannot be entertained."

There was no response she could give to that he wouldn't have seen as a challenge she had no intention of meeting, so she'd swallowed it all down. She'd accepted that for the first time in as long as she could remember, she was well and truly left to her own devices.

She'd gone out and lost herself in the ancient streets of the eternal city.

And it was out in the chaotic splendor of three thousand years of human habitation, losing herself on one street only to find her way back on another, that she realized she'd completely forgotten that Christmas was coming.

When normally this was her favorite time of year. The pressing dark, and the bright lights making joy against the night.

She found herself in a café in a bustling *piazza* one late afternoon, with a latte steaming gently at her elbow. It had been a wet day, cloudy and moody, and much too cold. She had left Dante in the capable hands of his caregivers. Who, if she was honest, she quite liked herself. And how could she argue with Pascal's desire that he receive that kind of attentive care when she herself had left him with the neighbor while she worked?

She couldn't. Or she would have, to be more precise, but she didn't quite dare.

There was something about Pascal here, prowling around his natural element, that made Cecilia feel as if she'd lost the ability to keep her feet on the ground. And not because it was cracking or rolling beneath her the way it felt sometimes, but because he'd taken it.

She blew out a breath as she looked at the bustling *piazza*, and all the Christmas lights and decorations that made it gleam no matter how dark or thick the incoming night. She could see the gleaming trees, done up proud and bright. She could hear the *zampognari* playing the mournful bagpipes, just as the Sicilian family had always claimed was tradition down south.

For a moment she felt very nearly at peace.

The abbey had always felt magical to her this time of year. The sisters had sung carols every morning, and the village itself had done itself up with trees draped in lights, wreaths on the doors and candles flickering in every window.

And suddenly, the fact she wasn't there to see it this year took her breath away.

Cecilia hadn't expected to miss home this much. It felt like a physical pain, wrenching and terrible, that she couldn't simply go outside, walk for five minutes no matter the weather and find herself in the cool, serene embrace of the abbey. That Mother Superior was not on hand for a dry comment, a bit of wisdom, or both.

She was well and truly on her own for the first time in her life, and Cecilia couldn't say she liked it.

Later, when she'd drained her coffee and left the café, she found her way home again through the tangle of streets, packed full of eras and people and cars that roared this way and that and parked in all directions. She only got lost twice, which she thought showed improvement, and found her way into Pascal's rambling three-story showcase of a home, resplendent in its usual state of modern, moneyed serenity. She was informed that her child was currently being fed and would soon after be bathed, before settling down into his evening routine.

They no longer pretended to ask her what she thought about this routine; they simply performed it.

Cecilia felt a surge of temper—or maybe it was fear—wash over her then. This was all part of Pascal's plan; she knew that. He was going out of his way to show her how easily he could keep her son from her, in retaliation. And she was letting it happen. Just standing here, letting him do his worst. She should storm into the middle of Dante's dinnertime, kick out all the staff members and reclaim her own son—

But even though she started across the polished marble of the foyer toward Dante's set of rooms, she stopped.

Because like it or not, Dante was having the time of his life. What right did she have to take something away from him because her feelings were hurt? Or because she felt lonely? Whether she liked it or not, he was the only son and heir of a very, very wealthy man. If this was how wealthy children were raised—and she certainly wouldn't know—who was she to deny him that?

She turned away from the hall that led to her son and headed for the nearest sitting room instead, so she could stare out the window at all the light and madness and *people* that made up the city she still couldn't believe she lived in now. The glass of the window was cold beneath her fingers, but she didn't lift her hand.

It wasn't as if she didn't see her own child. Dante always knew where she was and any of his new aides knew how to contact her if he needed her. She should congratulate herself on having raised such a confident child that he was happy to race around, immersing himself in his new life without giving her a second thought.

She would get there, she told herself. Maybe a little grimly. Somehow, she would find a way to be happy about all of this. For him.

"You look so glum, *cara*," came Pascal's low, insinuating voice from behind her.

As if the prospect amused him.

Cecilia took her time turning. It was early for him to be home, and she hated that she knew anything about his schedule. His routines. Because the real tragedy was that she'd started to anticipate his return every night. She could tell herself that it was because she grew ever more wary of him, and needed to buttress herself against him however possible...

But that wasn't quite true.

She faced him, entirely too aware that she didn't

feel any one thing when she looked at him. It was all mixed up together. Guilt and temper, her long-held anger, and beneath it all, that heat he could generate without even seeming to try.

She could still feel that kiss he'd given her on their wedding day. The way he'd claimed her mouth with his and taught her things she didn't want to know about herself, right there in front of the entirety of the church.

"I'm not glum at all," she told him now. "I was merely contemplating, as ever, the fact that you insisted on this marriage. And yet apparently have nothing for me to do here but wander the streets of Rome like a permanent tourist."

He stood in the doorway, still dressed in the sort of exquisitely cut suit he wore to work. And she really would have preferred the remove of a tabloid magazine, because the pages could only show him in two digestible dimensions. There was no way to sense the brooding power he wore. Or how impossible it was to look away from him. Or how she could *feel* him, like a switch flipped deep inside her.

Magazines made it clear he was beautiful. But the truth was, he was dangerous.

Because somehow it had been easier to hate him in the mountains. Here, where she was the one out of place, she found it a far more difficult prospect.

"You are my wife," he told her with that arrogance of his that should have repelled her. That it didn't was her secret shame. "That is your role. And do not kid yourself, it is a job. Do you think you can handle it?"

"Is this where you lecture me on what to wear and which fork to use?" she asked him, her voice like acid to her own ears. "You understand, it's not the comportment classes I object to. It's the teacher."

She didn't know who she had become here, over the course of these strange, confusing days in a city so large she couldn't make sense of it. And she was so completely within the power of this man, she couldn't make sense of herself.

Yet, she had the distinct impression *he* understood her all too well.

A small curve disturbed the stark line of his proud mouth. "I spent a significant amount of my time looking for the perfect wife. My requirements were simple. Poise, grace and aspirational elegance."

Cecilia hated the fact that sounded like a list of her failings.

"I'm a foundling who wanted to become a nun," she told him, the cold glass at her back. And far too much defensiveness in her voice. "A fallen woman who cleaned floors to care for her illegitimate child. There's no poise in that. And very little grace. And if you wanted elegance—well. You were the one who demanded this marriage."

"And here we are," Pascal murmured, moving farther into the room. "Just as I demanded."

The sitting room was one of several such pointless

areas in this jaw-droppingly immense place. As far as Cecilia could tell, the point of *so many rooms* in a home like this was to stock them all full of unnecessary things—antiques, art, that piano and whatever else shouted its status simply by existing. Because otherwise, what would be the point of having them? When she started thinking of this apartment like a museum, it made more sense.

But did that make her one more piece in his collection?

"We're well and truly married, Cecilia, in the eyes of God and man," he told her now. "There's no pretending otherwise."

"I wasn't pretending."

"Are you ready to take on your duties in that regard?" He was still smiling. She knew it was a warning. "I warn you, it may require that you spend less time idle and more time welded to my side, more or less."

"That is not appealing," she said crisply.

Pascal's smile widened. "You like it well enough in bed."

And really, she should have seen that coming.

But Cecilia had been going out of her way not to think about the nights here.

Pascal had insisted that she share his bed.

That first night she'd put Dante to bed, claiming he didn't like to sleep in new places. Only to curl up next to him because actually, she was the one who didn't want to sleep in this new place. She'd woken up to find herself being carried through this too-large place in her brand-new husband's arms, and had panicked.

"Calm yourself," he had told her briskly. "I am only carrying you to the marital bed, *cara*. I am not requiring you perform in it."

"I'm perfectly calm," she'd thrown at him, perhaps desperately. And when they'd reached the palatial suite of rooms that Pascal had said were his, it did not exactly relax her to discover that they were now hers, as well. "Put me down."

And she almost said *please*, but that would be begging.

Pascal had laughed, but he'd done what she asked. And she had been bleary-eyed and panicky, and still dressed in the clothes he'd set out for her to wear to travel that day. Clothes she had wanted to hate on principle, but couldn't. Because she had never in her life worn a sweater so soft, so warm. Or trousers that were not only comfortable to sit in for hours on end, but also seemed supernaturally incapable of wrinkling, even all these hours later. Even the shoes he'd provided had somehow managed to be both fashionable *and* comfortable.

Cecilia had looked at herself in too many mirrors today, whether in rest stops or in all the gleaming rooms of Pascal's absurd home, and she hadn't recognized herself at all. She didn't look like a simple woman who wanted to become a nun any longer. And she certainly didn't look like a country woman who cleaned to make her rent.

And the fact that all it took was a change of clothes to make her look like the sort of woman who really might belong in a place like this made her...uneasy.

"I have no intention of begging," she threw at him, because she couldn't say she liked the intent look in his eyes just then.

While she'd been curled around her son as if the child was her security blanket—instead of the other way around—Pascal had clearly showered, if his damp hair was anything to go by. And worse, was standing there before her wearing absolutely nothing but a pair of low-slung trousers.

Absolutely nothing.

"Did I ask you to beg?" he asked mildly. "Tonight?"

And Cecilia felt as if he'd lit her on fire. He was a perfectly formed, mouthwatering specimen of a man. She had thought so years ago—but it was even worse now. His scars tracked down his left side, where he'd sustained the most damage. But now they seemed like so much decoration. Not angry and livid, but simply scars. Markers on the map of his male beauty.

And the truth was, Cecilia wasn't sure she was equipped to handle this.

"Then why did you bring me in here?" she demanded.

"You will sleep in my bed," he told her as piti-less as ever, his black gaze unreadable. "And no, you will not come to my bed fully dressed. I will con-sider it an insult."

"But Dante—"

"The child will be monitored, naturally. By staff members paid for the purpose. Should he need you, they will rouse us both at once."

"But—"

"Cecilia." And she truly hated that soft tone of his, because it was Pascal at his most dangerous. And his most implacable. "I did not marry so that I could live apart from my wife."

"You married as a form of blackmail."

"I did not marry you to blackmail you." And she almost believed he meant that, until he shrugged. And that muscled wonder of his chest moved, mak-ing her mouth go dry. "But you would do well to re-member that this marriage is for my convenience, not yours."

Cecilia was entirely too aware of that. "I have al-ready given you far too much for one lifetime. I'm not giving you anything else."

And he had stood there, that faint smile on his sensual mouth, and something far too knowing in his dark gaze.

"I have already told you what will happen, but let me elaborate."

"Not on my account," she said, but he ignored her.

"You will beg me for my touch, and you will do so sooner rather than later. Believe this, if nothing else."

Then, just when she thought he would put his hands on her and carry her off against her will... Pascal did the exact opposite. He headed away from her instead, toward the vast platform bed that dominated the room they stood in, which she had been doing her level best not to look at.

Cecilia watched, surprised and a little bit put out, as he climbed into the bed and sprawled there, like Roman emperors of old.

"Do you need a nap before you finish threatening me?" she asked. With perhaps a bit too much emotion in her voice.

"I want you in this bed," Pascal told her in a dark tone that made her melt, then burn. "But I'm not going to wrestle you into it. If you go and sleep somewhere else, I will simply come find you, bring you back and set you on your own two feet. Right there. Until you come to your senses and get into bed beside me. The question you should ask yourself, Cecilia, is how tired are you tonight? How many times do you wish to do this?"

"I'm exhausted," she had managed to say. "I don't want to do this at all."

"Then if I were you, I would come to bed. Now. Instead of performing a grand charade that will end the same way no matter what you do."

And Cecilia had believed him. She had walked

stiffly from the room, but not to escape him. Only to tend to herself after such a long trip—and the far longer walk down that aisle that she still couldn't believe had happened. She'd washed her face, then changed into the only thing she'd brought with her that bore any resemblance to appropriate sleepwear. It was the slip she'd worn beneath her dress, and it seemed silly to put it on to sleep in.

But the alternative to that was to crawl into Pascal's bed naked.

And that was clearly impossible.

She stalked back out into the bedroom to find Pascal typing something into his phone, looking wholly at ease. She glared at him, but he didn't look up. Still, she was sure she could feel his eyes on her as she skirted the foot of the bed, then stood there for a moment on the opposite side.

Cecilia understood what he was playing at, suddenly. This was the first surrender. He could easily have picked her up and tossed her on the bed. He could have kissed her and made her forget her own name.

But he was making her do this. He was making her do this *to herself.*

She should have turned and run into one of the many other rooms. One of them was bound to have a lock—

But she didn't. She climbed into bed and lay as close to the edge as she could get without toppling off. Rigid and resentful, like a martyr at the pyre.

He turned off the lights not long after, and settled in. Cecilia waited. Every muscle inside her body was tense, prepared for him to reach over, take liberties, go back on his word...

But instead, and in an indecently short span of time that suggested his mind was not similarly pre-occupied, she heard his breath go even.

He had fallen asleep.

Leaving her there with her fingers gripping the edge of the bed as if she'd expected to be dragged off somewhere at any moment. Long into the night.

The next morning she'd woken up because she was so deliciously warm she'd thought she might find herself curled up on the surface of the sun.

But it was much worse than that.

She was sprawled out all over Pascal, her legs tangled with his. Her hair all over his chest. Her mouth there against his hard muscles.

Cecilia had sucked in a breath of pure horror, then threw herself to the side, hoping against hope that he was still—

"You still feel like silk and longing," he told her, his voice rich with sleep, amusement and something far darker that pulsed inside her. "When you beg me, *cara*, I will make you sob. Over and over and over again."

"In your dreams," she'd hissed at him, already scrambling out of the bed and heading for the bathroom suite.

"Please, *cara*." And his gaze was so hungry she nearly tripped. It made her heart pound even as she felt herself melt, then ache low in her belly and between her legs. "My dreams are far more demanding."

Every night since had been the same thing.

If Pascal was home when Cecilia went to bed, he stayed far off on his side. He made no move toward her. And they still ended up in that breathless tangle each morning. If he was out when she went to bed, she would always wake up with a start when he climbed in, sure that *this time* he would trespass over that invisible line that ran down the center of the bed...but he never did.

And it made no difference. They still woke up in a knot.

Cecilia was beginning to understand that her body simply wanted him. And didn't much care how she got him.

Standing there in one of his many salons tricked out in priceless objects, nothing but glass at her back and her uncertain future before her, the last thing Cecilia wanted to feel was breathless. She glared at him.

"No clever response to that?" Pascal asked almost idly. "I'm disappointed."

"Is that part of my punishment? It's not enough that you force me to sleep in the same bed with you, you must also taunt me about it?"

"I'm not punishing you, *cara*. You would know."

"I can't imagine how an actual punishment would differ from this," she threw back at him.

"For one thing," he replied, too easily, "it will be public as well as private."

But she had been a nun who turned up pregnant. What could he possibly do to her that she hadn't already lived through, more or less happily?

"Public humiliation is hardly good for Dante. Who is supposed to be the point of all this, isn't he? How quickly you forget."

"I forget nothing," he said, and there was a note in his voice that made her neck prickle in warning.

She didn't pretend to understand this man she'd married. There was something about the way he watched her, hungry and angry at once, that unsettled her too deeply. She hurried from the room, determined to reclaim at least some part of Dante's evening routine after all.

Because she needed a touchstone. She needed *something*.

She dismissed his staff, then read him a story, and kissed him as he drifted off to sleep. As if nothing had changed but the size of his bedroom.

And it was then, in the darkness while her little boy dreamed, that she had to accept the truth she'd been wrestling with. Her heart was not the least bit worried about Dante. Not only would he thrive here, and was—there was no doubt in her mind that Pascal loved him.

With the same reckless, heedless and instantaneous devotion that she herself had felt when he'd been tucked there inside her.

Seeing them together…did things to her. Watching the man who so overwhelmed her squat down to talk seriously, yet kindly, with her child—with *their* child—made her feel something like giddy.

And she might have told herself that she had come to Rome to save Dante from him, but she knew tonight that wasn't true. She wasn't afraid, on any level, that Pascal would harm her son.

She was far more concerned that Pascal would harm her instead.

And the following morning she woke up to find him gone. It felt like a premonition come true—a notion she tried to shake off.

"I'm afraid you cannot go out today," the housekeeper told her sorrowfully when she made to leave after her breakfast. "There are paparazzi camped out around the building, and Signor Furlani would prefer you not give them any more ammunition."

"Ammunition?" she queried. Then blinked. "Paparazzi?"

The housekeeper delivered her the stack of morning papers. And there it was. A picture of the two of them together. Their wedding. Pascal leaning into her, his mouth hovering above hers.

And Cecilia hardly recognized herself. She

looked…flushed and starry-eyed. Like the silly girl she'd been when she'd first met him.

She hated that the picture existed. Much less that it was now…out there, for the entire world to dissect. It felt like a kind of death. Something far worse than a shaming.

But far worse than being exposed like that herself was the fact that Dante was splashed across all those papers, too.

His sweet face was there in bright color.

Furlani claims his son! one headline screamed.

And then, just beneath it, *thumbs his nose at father once again.*

Just like that, it all became clear.

Cecilia felt as if a truck hit her. She sat in the breakfast room, her ears ringing, feeling sick to her stomach. She read every single article she could find, then pulled out her mobile to look for even more.

And every word she read was like a nail into her heart.

"How did Signor Furlani leave the building this morning?" she asked the housekeeper when she could speak. When the betrayal was an agony inside her instead of wholly incapacitating her.

"Well, *signora*, he took a car. But—"

"Then get me a car," Cecilia demanded.

And that was how she found herself sitting in the backseat of a luxury vehicle she couldn't have named if her life depended on it, hiding behind tinted windows while men with twisted faces pounded their fists and open palms against the sides. This was the pit her husband had thrown their son into. All to score points with his own father.

None of this had been about Dante.

Or about you.

Pascal's offices were done up in low-slung furniture and steel accents. It made her think of the man she'd married. So beautiful and austere on the outside, and nothing but steel and lies within. There was no comfort to be found here. Or in him.

His secretary met her after a short, undignified squabble with his front desk, and led her back through the gleaming maze of offices separated by nothing but panes of glass. He took her directly to the center, where a group of men stood around a long table in yet another glass enclosure.

Cecilia was starting to rethink her urge to come here and tell her husband exactly what she thought of his little games, but it was too late. Because Pascal's secretary knocked twice on the great glass door, then swept it open. And every stuffy, officious man in that room turned to stare at her.

But it was only Pascal's gaze that she felt.

And her husband did not leap from the leather chair where he lounged as if he was at a café, whiling away the day. He did not look the least bit surprised to see her, and in fact, when his gaze met hers and held he looked even more lazy than he had a moment before.

She had the strangest notion that he was the one who felt out of place, always. Even here.

"May I present the woman in question, gentlemen," he drawled as if he'd invited her here. "Cecilia Furlani, in the flesh. Not a publicity stunt as you have accused me. But my wife."

CHAPTER NINE

PASCAL KNEW THAT Cecilia could ruin him, here and now.

All she would have to do was contradict him and the gauzy, romantic story he'd delivered to the papers, filled with smoke and mirrors about the two of them and their son. She could simply open up her mouth and tell the assembled men any story she liked about their marriage—and the real timeline of events. She could tell them who he had been six years ago and how he had left her to have and raise his child on her own. That truth would do the trick with this particular group of hypocrites quite nicely. It would give them all the ammunition they needed to start making noises about *moral questions*.

Even if she didn't wish to tell the truth—even if she decided to editorialize at will—it didn't matter. It would do the same damage. Worse, in this room with too many eyes on them, he couldn't stop her.

They wanted a reason to call him unfit. All she had to do was give them one.

And Pascal couldn't think of any particular reason why she wouldn't go ahead and do just that.

He stared at the face of the woman who had haunted him when she was not in his life, and was something far worse than a ghost now that she was. Ghosts only came out at night. But Cecilia haunted him always. Bright light of day through winter dark, then back again.

How had he imagined it would be different once he'd put his ring on her finger?

He knew why she was here, barging into his office with that furious look on her face. Oh, yes, he knew. He had told her she would beg, and he'd been arrogantly certain that all it would take was one night in his bed. Maybe two.

But he should have known better. He should have understood who Cecilia was. Not the soft, fragile girl he'd met all those years ago and had made into a monument of sweet innocence in his head, but the far tougher and more self-possessed woman who'd stared him down in a church and thrown his fatherhood in his face.

Perhaps the truth was she was both. But either way, Cecilia did not bend.

Meanwhile, Pascal felt as if he might break.

He had told himself it was time to make announcements about his marriage because it was high time he take charge of his unruly board and cut off their favorite line of dissent. It made business sense, he'd assured himself. And it was only a few days to Christmas, which meant the interest in the story would dissipate quickly as everyone turned their attention to their holidays. He'd had the distinct sensation that planting those newspaper stories had been an act of reclaiming himself somehow. Returning to form.

Or maybe, something sly suggested inside him, *you knew exactly what reaction she would have.*

Because despite his best efforts, Pascal was the one who was falling apart, little as he wished to admit that.

He was the one who woke again and again in the night, every time she shifted to get closer to him. She did it in her sleep. He was the one who held her, staring into the dark and wondering what the hell had happened to him. Where was the man who had built his entire life as a shrine to revenge? Where was the Pascal Furlani who would do anything at all—and had, happily—to live his life *at* the father who had always ignored him and pretended he didn't exist?

Most of Pascal's adult life had been an exercise in proving that he did, in fact, exist.

In his father's face, one way or another, in a way that could not be ignored.

And he didn't know how to reconcile that part of him with a man who wanted nothing more than the woman who only suffered his touch while she was asleep to want him while she was awake.

As desperately as he wanted her.

"Your new husband has been telling us romantic stories about the two of you, *signora*," said Pascal's least favorite board member, Carlo Buccio, with his silver hair, fussy beard and the cane he used as a prop. Carlo was forever looking for ways to take more away from Pascal. To render him little more than a figurehead, because that was the thing about power. People always wanted more of it. And better still, they wanted others around them to have less. He and his mustachioed sidekick, Massimo Pugliese, prided themselves on being thorns in Pascal's side.

He recalled, then, that they had also taken a field trip to the mountains. No doubt they were annoyed that their version of Pascal's life hadn't been splashed all over the tabloids first.

"Surely it cannot all have been fairy tales," Massimo chimed in, right on cue.

Pascal could do nothing but watch a series of complicated emotions chase themselves across Cecilia's face. He gritted his teeth as she shifted her condemning glare from him and looked at the rest of the assembled men.

But to his surprise, she laughed.

"Romance and fairy tales in a corporate boardroom?" Cecilia asked lightly. "How inappropriate.

Why on earth would such a private matter be discussed at all?"

And something in Pascal hummed a bit at that, amusement and admiration at once, though it hardly wiped away the tension that gripped him.

Because this was no trophy wife, clearly. This was no airheaded little bimbo, whose worth was in the picture she made while hanging on a rich man's arm. Not that Cecilia didn't make a pretty picture, but the glory of his wife, Pascal understood then as he never had before, was that she exuded that same matter-of-fact grace that her Mother Superior did. It wasn't holier than thou. It was the way she held herself and the frankness of her violet gaze. She didn't simper. She didn't avert her eyes. She didn't shrink down with so many male gazes trained upon her.

She stood there in his glass and stone meeting room as a kind of beacon. Of what was right, no matter what.

It was subtle, but effective. There was a mass clearing of throats and shuffling feet, as a room full of powerful men readjusted themselves to what Pascal could only consider the enduring power of the nunnery.

Cecilia might not be a nun. She might not have made it through her novitiate period, thanks to him. But that didn't mean she hadn't been convent-bred—or that she couldn't wield it like a weapon when she chose.

He had been so focused on claiming her that he hadn't stopped to fully appreciate what she brought to the table.

"I was under the seemingly quaint impression that one's private life was just that." And Cecilia might have been standing there as if she was addressing the room, but Pascal had no illusions. He knew that she was speaking directly to him when she said that. She even turned that gaze of hers on him again. *"Private."*

"Privacy is for far less powerful people, *signora*," Massimo said with his patented obsequiousness.

Cecilia merely turned a bland gaze his way. "How powerful is my five-year-old son?"

"Pascal has been filling us in on this…secret relationship of yours," Carlo said, his voice ripe with insinuation.

Pascal tensed even further in his chair at the head of the long table. Because she was clearly not happy with him, and here was her chance to vent her spleen. Here was her chance to get back everything she imagined had been taken from her. All she had to do was tell the story of what had actually happened, with all the bitterness and hurt she'd shown when she'd told the same story to him. These men would twist to suit themselves—and what they wanted to believe, so long as it advanced their position at his expense—and Pascal would have no choice but to go to war. Again.

And he saw the exact moment Cecilia understood that.

She blinked, and he could see her violet gaze turn canny. Considering. She turned it on him, and not for the first time, he wondered what she saw. If he had ever haunted her the way she did him.

He couldn't bear the tension and so he stood to break it, smoothing his hand down the front of his suit. He kept his gaze intent on Cecilia.

And then he waited for her to betray him, the way everyone who had ever vowed to love him had, sooner or later. His mother. His father. Now his wife, who had stood in a church and made her vows, though he'd told himself then that he hadn't believed them.

Because, of course, he'd forced her to that altar. He'd made her take those vows.

But in the dark of night, with her hair a fragrant cloud across his chest and her soft curves pressed into his side, he'd wanted to believe that every word she'd uttered before the priest had been true.

He'd wanted it more than could possibly be wise. Or healthy.

And all of that led here. Where he, a man who had callously betrayed anyone who ventured close to him in turn, waited in a moment that stretched on and on into eternity, for his just deserts.

Lord knew Pascal was full up on just deserts. He'd been choking them down his whole life.

Cecilia's lovely mouth curved, slightly. Her eyes flashed.

And Pascal was already calculating his response. Damage control. Counterattacks. The best way to undercut whatever she was about to say—

"I beg your pardon," Cecilia said, and again her voice was mild in the same way Mother Superior's always was. Kind, almost. And underneath it, absolute steel. It took Pascal a moment to notice she was not looking at him—she was looking at Carlo. "Something that is a secret to you, *signor*, is not necessarily a secret to the people involved. What a strange question. Would you like to share with the room every detail of your private relationships?"

For a moment Pascal couldn't process that.

It wasn't only that she'd taken aim at one of the most notorious philanderers in Rome, whose complicated series of mistresses left him eternally open to tabloid speculation. As did his wife's equally comprehensive selection of lovers, many of whom she paraded beneath Carlo's nose.

He supposed that it wouldn't have mattered whom she'd asked that question. There wasn't a man in this room whose private life could bear the scrutiny. It was only Pascal, who had lacked a wife and had insisted upon a social life over the past few years, who was subject to these patronizing reviews of his intimate relations.

It took a long moment for her question to penetrate, and for him to admire the way Cecilia had done it—so beautifully shifting the conversation away from Pascal.

It took another kick of his heart for him to understand the far more salient point.

She had not betrayed him when she'd had the chance.

She had not betrayed him.

And it was as if the floor dropped away from beneath his feet. As if the world shuddered to a halt and then stood still for a moment. Still and impossibly, confoundingly airless.

He felt tight, everywhere. As if he had exploded, and then had contained each and every shard, binding all the jagged edges inside himself.

He couldn't breathe. He couldn't *think*.

She had not *betrayed him.*

Cecilia turned her gaze back to his, then, and everything else fell away.

There was only this. Those violet eyes filled with temper, sadness, sheer fury and something else he couldn't name.

There was only her, standing there in the clothes he'd bought for her, looking like every dream he'd ever had of the perfect wife.

Because the only dream he'd ever had, in all these years, had been her.

Her. Cecilia.

The only person alive who had not betrayed him at the first opportunity.

The fact that they were still standing here in full view of his entire shark tank full of grasping directors impressed itself upon him, then, as if from a great distance. Pascal moved from the table, distantly amazed that his body still worked. That the explosion that was still rolling through him in the form of aftershocks had not, in fact, taken him out at the knees. That while he might feel every one of those jagged edges, they were not necessarily visible.

His head was spinning. He could feel the thump of his heart, and the tightness in his gut. He expected his hands to be shaking when he reached out to usher Cecilia back through the door, but they weren't.

Somehow they weren't.

He excused himself, and her, or maybe he sang a happy song—he would never know. It was all noise and wonder and *her* inside him.

More than that, he didn't care what any of his board members thought. Not any longer.

He led Cecilia out of the meeting room. And for the first time since he'd built it, Pascal cursed the bright, open office he'd been so proud of before. He led her through a maze of glass and too many eyes, winding his way back to his own office, when all he wanted was privacy. A closed door. A place to hide and figure out what the hell had just happened.

When they reached his office at last, he ignored

Guglielmo and motioned for Cecilia to precede him inside. She did, her back in a beautiful straight line as she moved ahead of him, then kept walking across the floor toward the bank of windows.

For a moment he could only stare. Ancient, beautiful Rome outside the glass and his Cecilia within. It made his chest hurt.

"Why did you do that?"

He threw the question at her, his voice a rough, low sort of growl as he closed the door behind him. Then locked it, for safe measure. And he hit the button that darkened the glass all around them, making his walls distinctly opaque and private at last.

But he didn't move from the door.

"A better question is why you did it," she replied, keeping her back to him. "Why would you share pictures of our wedding with the world? Why would you tell them lies about us? And why—" And that was when she turned, her violet eyes dark with that fury again. "Why on earth would you give them pictures of Dante, Pascal?"

And for a blistering moment it was as if he couldn't remember why he'd made the very distinct choices he had. As if all she needed to do was look at him with her otherworldly eyes, and he was lost.

But he refused to accept that. *He refused.*

He opened his mouth to give her his reasons. It wasn't as if he didn't have them, or hadn't suspected he might be called upon to do just that. After all, he had long since made an art out of acting the bastard he knew he was. Biologically and otherwise.

Yet somehow, beneath that steady violet gaze, he found he couldn't do it.

Cecilia had not betrayed him, but he couldn't say the same.

He remembered his own mother then. Wailing on the floor after another rejection from his father.

We are the dirt beneath his feet, Marissa would cry.

Pascal had spent so long exulting in that status, turning it around and making it a virtue, that he'd forgotten the truth of it. He could call it whatever he liked. He could dress it up and use it to his advantage, and he had.

But dirt was still dirt.

He looked at Cecilia, his beautiful wife who had been wholly innocent until she'd met him. And he knew that sooner or later, the longer he kept her with him, all he would do was tarnish her, too.

He would cover her in dirt. Hadn't he already done so?

She had been pure, and he had corrupted her. She had built herself a life after he'd left, putting together the pieces of a fall from grace right there in the abbey where she'd been raised, and making it something beautiful. And he had ruined that, too.

He had forced her into coming with him. Threatened her with the loss of her child.

That was who he was. A man who had never known one of his parents and had suffered for it, and yet had thrown himself wholeheartedly into pressuring the only parent his own son had ever known into doing as he wished. And more, making her believe that he would take the child away from her.

Dirt into dirt. Dirt forever, staining him no matter how exquisitely he dressed these days. Dirt was who he was.

The distance between them seemed far more vast and unconquerable than simply the span of his office floor.

He wished that he'd done something on one of those torturous nights when he'd lain awake, holding her in his arms and wondering how he would keep from breaking. He wished he'd simply turned, set his mouth against her skin, and let it happen.

Where would they be now?

But of course he hadn't done it. Pascal preferred to armor everything, especially if it would have been better to cherish it. If there was a gift that could be given, he could be counted upon to break it first. To make it into a challenge instead.

Because going to one war or another was all he knew how to do.

That and cover any good thing he found in his own brand of dirt and kick it around a few times, just for good measure.

If he was any kind of man at all, he would fall to

his knees here and now, and beg her the way he'd told her she would beg him.

If he was something more than a grim monument to a whole life spent avenging himself on a man who stoutly refused to care one way or the other, he would have thanked her.

Loved her. Cherished her.

Just like the vows he'd made himself, there in the only place on this planet where he'd ever briefly toyed with the idea that he could be more than just an angry man. A good one, say. Or simply...whole.

But he couldn't do it.

He couldn't make himself do it.

"I did it because that is who I am," he told her, and his voice sounded like the old man he would become. Bitter. Old. Calcified by his own grim march toward the darkness. "I seek my own ends, Cecilia. Always. I know no other way."

She sucked in a shocked sort of breath as if he'd punched her, so he kept going.

"Nothing and no one is safe," he growled. "I will use you. I will use our child. I will use anything and everything if it serves my purpose. Did you expect something else of a man who threatened you as I have?"

And he braced himself for tears. Temper. It was one thing to stand and deliver his own character assassination. It would be something else again to hear her do it. But he told himself he was prepared.

Because it wasn't as if, no matter what she said, it wouldn't be the truth. She took a few steps toward him, and then stopped, almost as if she hadn't meant to move. He wondered, almost idly, if she would strike him. If he would let her.

But she didn't raise her hands. Instead, Cecilia studied him, for the span of a long, hard breath. Then another.

She took another step toward him, and he couldn't help himself. He could only admire how quickly and easily she had taken to his new role of hers, however little she'd enjoyed her time in Rome. Even in a temper, as today, she had dressed from the wardrobe he'd provided her. Her honey-colored hair was twisted back into an effortless chignon. It only emphasized her unusual eyes. She wore a wool dress that hugged her lithe curves and a pair of boots in butter-soft leather. She looked simple, yet elegant. She always had.

The only difference now was that the clothes she wore enhanced what was already there, in a way the ragged, torn clothes she'd worn in her role as a cleaner never could.

It was due to his own arrogance that he'd ever imagined she was within his reach.

Accordingly, he stood where he was, ready for anything she might throw at him.

"That's a dark picture you paint," was all she said.

"Of a dark and remorseless man, incapable of changing himself for the better."

He couldn't read her expression. Or her voice. He could feel his pulse, rocketing through him too hard. Too fast. "It is an accurate portrait."

"You say that as if I did not already know exactly who you were, Pascal."

His lips thinned at that. "Then I should not have to tell you these things. But I will." He told himself his throat was not dry. He was not too tense. That none of those things were happening to him, because he should have been perfectly calm. "If I were you, Cecilia, I would go."

"Go?"

"Take the child. Leave. You were right all along—this was a mistake."

The words felt to him like a thunderclap. Intense and huge. Impossible to ignore.

And everyone knew that when thunder rumbled, the storm could not be far behind.

"I could do that." But Cecilia's voice was too quiet. Too soft, and yet not weak at all. Steel serenity, and he knew precisely where she'd learned it. Her violet gaze held his. "Or instead, I could beg."

Beg.

The word seemed to take over his head, his chest, *him*. It seemed to pour in from the sprawling, ancient city outside to fill the room. It was in his blood, bruising and powerful.

I could beg, she had said.

And he remembered, again that moment on a frozen field high up in the mountains. He remembered how deeply and fervently he had wanted all the things he knew he couldn't have. Because he had never had them.

His woman. His son.

A family.

I could beg, she'd said.

He knew better. He was Pascal Furlani, not another, softer man. And all he knew how to do was struggle. How to fight. How to punish the world in general and his father in particular for failing him.

But Cecilia *lived*.

She had nursed him back to life, literally. She had given birth to a brand-new life, Dante.

She was life. Love. All the things that Pascal did not dare permit himself to imagine he could ever, ever have—

"This is me begging," she said, her voice musical. Impossible.

And then she made it worse by sinking down onto her knees, right there before him. With all the ease and grace of a dancer or a queen, as if she wasn't the one capitulating.

Or as if, he thought in some kind of a daze, as if surrender cost her nothing.

When he was certain it would destroy him.

"Pascal," she said, her remarkable eyes locked

to his. "I want you to make me your wife, in every possible way. I'm begging you to do it. Right now."

And Pascal had been born a lost cause. Accordingly, he'd lost himself for years, as an avocation. He reveled in that dirt, that stain, and had only imagined himself found when he'd nearly died on a distant mountain. Until this woman smiled at him, then nursed him whole.

He was lost in that gaze of hers, violet and sure.

And maybe the truth was that he was already lost. That he had been for six years now, and counting.

So he pulled her to her feet, then swept her into his arms, taking her mouth in a kind of fury.

And lost himself for good.

CHAPTER TEN

CECILIA UNDERSTOOD EVERYTHING in a sweet, sudden rush. A glorious flash of flame and longing, while his mouth moved on hers and remade the world again.

It was all about fear.

She wrapped her arms around him and let him bear her down to the ground, sighing in happiness as he fit that exquisite body of his to the length of hers, proving yet again how well he fit.

How beautifully they had always fit, just like this.

Fear was why she hadn't looked harder for him, when she could have. Fear was what had kept her in the mountains guarding her child, instead of taking the harder, scarier route and facing him six years ago. Five years ago.

Or any day since.

And fear was what had made him do what he'd done. She got that now. Because revenge was what Pascal knew. It was easier. Anger was far more palatable than those hot, confusing mornings when they woke up wound up in each other. If he made her angry, she understood, he could fight her. He could make demands, issue threats.

He could reduce what was happening between them—what had always been happening between them—to a simple little battle.

But Pascal was not a bully. She knew that like she knew her own heart. It wasn't her weakness he was after, it was her strength. Weakness would have wrecked him. It was her strength that allowed him to treat her like an adversary.

Because adversaries could not be hurt. Adversaries fought.

And if they were fighting, they couldn't be afraid.

Cecilia understood all of it as he kissed her, his mouth hot and wicked and *perfect*. She understood it as she kissed him back with all the fire and need he'd taught her.

Pascal pulled back and stripped himself out of his jacket, his shirt. Cecilia took the opportunity to pull off the dress she wore, leaving her in nothing but a bra, her panties and her boots.

His eyes darkened, and that sensual mouth of his firmed. And he looked at her as if he wanted nothing more than to get his mouth on every last centimeter of her. As if he might die if he didn't do precisely that. Now.

"You kill me," he growled, the sensual menace

in his voice making her shudder with *want*. "Every time, you kill me."

His hands were on her, like bright hot flame and searing madness, testing the shape of her breasts and then gripping her hips to haul her toward him again.

And his mouth on hers was a revelation.

So good, so right, that Cecilia understood why she'd been refusing herself the very thing she'd given so freely six years ago. *She was afraid.*

Of what it would do to her. And what it would do to her life. Because the truth was, having sex with Pascal had already changed her entire world once. What would he do this time?

But she already knew. Sex wasn't the danger here. Sex wasn't going to ruin her and wreck her, stalking her across the years until she found him again. Love was.

And the simple truth was, she had never stopped loving Pascal.

She wasn't sure she ever would.

So Cecilia kissed him back, pouring the years they'd been apart into it. The fear and the loneliness, and more than that, all her dreams. All her joy. The flavor of the life she'd lived away from him, and all the secret hopes she hid inside her that this new life they'd started together would bloom despite their best efforts to pretend it was a misery.

She kissed him and she kissed him. And when he got to his feet again, then pulled her up, she followed him blindly. Greedily. He carried her over to the long, low sofa, and lay her down upon it. She watched, breathing too hard, as he kicked off his trousers and the boxer briefs he wore beneath them, then bared himself to her gaze at last.

For a moment she lay there, sprawled out in abandon. She simply looked at him.

Because she could never get enough of *looking* at this man.

His scars, his muscles. All together, the devastating masculine beauty that was Pascal Furlani, the only man she'd ever touched. The only man she'd ever loved.

As far as Cecilia was concerned, the only man there was. Full stop.

His black eyes glittered. His shoulders were wide enough to cling to, forever. Between his legs, the hardest part of him stood tall, proud.

And she loved him.

There was nothing else to understand, but that.

She lifted her hands toward him, and she smiled. "How much begging do I have to do?"

"Take off your bra," he ordered her, his voice a gritty rasp.

Cecilia levered herself up and reached around to obey him, pulling off one cup, then the other. Then she bared her breasts to him, his gaze alone making her nipples pull tight. She let out a shaky sort of breath as sensation washed over her.

"And your panties," he said. His hard mouth curled in one corner, making her shake even more. "But you can leave the boots on."

She didn't know why that struck her as so unbearably delicious, but it did. She hurried to comply, pulling her panties over her hips, then fighting to get them over the leather of her boots.

And when she was done, she was on her feet again, standing before him. On display in a way that should have made her think twice.

But she was thoroughly his. That was what she thought about.

His black eyes burned. His mouth curved even more.

And then he was reaching for her, pulling her close and then lifting her up.

Cecilia held on to his wide, hard shoulders as she crossed her legs around his waist. Then she moaned as he shifted her farther, lifting her up and then holding her there—stretched taught above the hardest part of him at last.

His face was close to hers, drawn into a fiercely sensual mask that made her whole body hurt. In the best possible way.

"Beg me," he whispered.

His expression was raw. His black eyes were lit with a golden need. And Cecilia felt the same inside as if she'd been scraped clean. Hollowed out.

And all that was left was this. *Him*.

This thing that had always been between them, coiled tight and wild and impossible to ignore— though they'd both tried.

Love.

There was no other word for it.

She dug her fingers into his shoulders and she gazed down into his face, taut and hard with the force of that same rampant need that was charging through her, leaving her molten hot and nearly bursting out of her own skin.

"Please, Pascal," she whispered, filled with the exquisite joy of a surrender that felt like a triumph. "Please."

And then he thrust into her, deep.

He impaled her upon him, and for a moment they both froze, swamped with the same wild sensation.

The heat. The sweet, slick perfection.

Home, Cecilia thought. *Love.*

Yes.

And she didn't know which parts of that she'd said out loud.

But then it didn't matter.

Pascal was bringing her back down to the couch again, bracing himself above her as they both adjusted and he slid in even deeper.

Her mouth was in the crook of his neck, and her teeth were at his shoulder.

And he was surging inside her, pounding into her again and again and again as if they would die this way, or die if they didn't, or die and be reborn and do this dance forever, just like this.

Cecilia met him. She was a part of him. She kept her legs wrapped around his hips and met his every thrust.

She remembered the glory of this six years ago. The brief flash of pain, then nothing but need and longing made flesh.

And it was better now. Deeper, harder.

It was too much and not enough. It was everything and yet they strained together for more.

Pascal did something with his hips, making her throw back her head to ride it out. Then he bent his head to take one tight nipple into his mouth, and she was done. She shattered. Her whole body clenched hard around his, then shook.

She shook and shook and shook.

But still he kept going, pounding her through one shivering climax, then straight back into the fire to burn toward another.

Cecilia held on to him for dear life, and she loved him. She cried, she called out his name and she let herself drown in the exquisite flames, the remarkable burn, as it mounted inside her all over again.

But it wasn't until she started to shudder again, her thighs clamping down hard on him, that he finally lost that deep, measured pace that he'd been using to drive her wild.

And for a moment it was all speed and fury, beautiful and deep.

Then Pascal was shattering, too, her name on his lips as he lost himself inside her at last.

And Cecilia thought, with perfect clarity, *this*.

She wanted this. All of this. The storm, beautiful and elemental, that was this man and the passion that had sparked between them from the first. From long before she'd understood what it was that called her to his side in that clinic. She wanted the thunder of the need she felt for him, the lightning that was their passion that felt like its own fury, like pain and sometimes like loss. And the rain that followed, but brought life to the world.

It had brought her their son.

She wanted that storm with everything she had, everything she was. It was worth the price she'd paid. It was worth anything.

She reached up and took Pascal's face between her hands. She felt his scars on one side, the evidence that he could overcome anything. She searched his gaze, black-gold and unfocused, though he slowly focused in on her.

And for a moment it was as if he was new.

As if the rain had washed them both clean, so they could start again.

Cecilia wasn't afraid anymore. Not to beg for what she wanted, and not to set free the things that roared inside her, desperate to get out. And certainly not of the man still lodged so deep inside her, it was hard to remember they were different people.

"I love you," she said, very distinctly. "I love you, Pascal."

The effect on him was instant and electric.

And not good.

His brows clapped together. His eyes flashed. He scowled at her, and then he moved back. He disengaged himself from her body and pulled himself away, a lot as if she'd scalded him.

Cecilia stayed where she was; propping herself up on one elbow she watched him stalk away from her.

It wasn't as if there was any angle on that beautiful body of his that she didn't admire.

She watched him shove a hand through his hair. Then he stood with his hands on his hips, glaring toward his windows as if he could level Rome with the force of his temper. She wasn't surprised when his hand drifted down to stroke the scars on his jaw.

"I love you, Pascal," she said again, so there could be no mistake.

And when he turned back to level that same glare at her, she only smiled. She sat up, but she did absolutely nothing to cover herself. She simply smiled back at him.

And he looked at her as if she'd taken a swing at him.

"I've always loved you," she said as if she was confiding a great secret. "Even when I hated you the most, there was a little part inside me that hoped that you would come back. Because that was what would make it right, no matter what had happened. I just loved you, and I wanted to be with you, even when I would have sworn up and down I didn't. And when you did come back, what terrified me the most was that all that love hadn't gone anywhere. It was just waiting—"

"It is impossible," he told her then, sounding as if he was chewing glass as he spoke. "You must know this."

"Which part?" She watched him stalk over to grab his trousers and wondered if he was having as much trouble concentrating as she was. What with all the nudity in the room. "Because I assure you, it's actually quite easy to love. You just do it."

Pascal didn't say anything. He dressed quickly and quietly, and when she didn't rush to do the same, he lifted one of those dark brows at her direction.

Cecilia sighed, then took her time refastening her bra. She stepped into her panties, pulled them into place, and then she took a very long time indeed to wander over across the office floor and pick up her dress. When she finally shimmied it over her head and back into place, he was gritting his teeth so hard that she was fairly surprised his jaw didn't shatter.

She smiled. Pascal did not.

"I told you that you would beg, and you did," he said darkly. "But I see no reason whatsoever to drag out the rest of this charade. I will have my secretary contact you and you can hammer out the details with him."

"What details?"

"We've already covered this," he said, but though his voice was as commanding as ever, his eyes told a different story. It was as if he was so wounded he'd… gone numb. And had no idea that he was staggering about while missing a limb. "Take Dante. Go back to your mountains. You're safer there."

"I love those mountains," Cecilia said. "I always will. But they're not the only thing I love."

"I heard you." His voice could have cut stone in half, and she was somewhat surprised she wasn't in pieces herself. "I don't need to hear it again."

But she had decided to stop being afraid. No matter what.

"I want everything, Pascal," she told him. "I want a real marriage. I want a real family. I want a real life. With you."

"And you deserve those things." He sounded stiff, but she could see the torment in his eyes. "But I cannot give them to you."

She made herself laugh. "You're one of the richest, most powerful men in Italy. You can give me whatever you want to give me."

"Cecilia—"

"Think of it. *Real life*, Pascal. No threats, no lies. No secrets. Just us."

And she could see the storm break in him then. She lifted her hand toward him—but he stepped back as if he was afraid that she would tear him in two.

As if she already had.

"I can't be *real*," he threw at her, and her heart broke at the sound of his voice. So ragged. So raw. "I wouldn't know how to begin. I was born broken and I've only gotten worse."

And she wanted to put her hands on him more than she wanted her next breath. She wanted to gather him to her, and soothe him somehow. She wanted to shout at him, shake him.

But she knew he wouldn't let her do any of that.

Instead, she tried to smile. "All you have to do is choose love, Pascal," she told him quietly, but with every bit of truth she knew right there in her voice. "Choose me. Just once."

Six years ago he'd run. And she understood why he had, why he'd believed he had no other choice. But understanding the past didn't change it; it could only—if they were lucky—change the future.

"Just once," she whispered.

But Pascal was shaking his head. And she wanted to scream at him, beg him all over again, but he looked tortured. Ripped apart.

"I can't," he gritted out. And then he stood a little straighter, lifting his head to meet her stricken gaze head-on. "If that means you have to leave me, I understand. I told you. I think you should."

She had been asleep the last time he'd left her. And maybe that had been a kindness after all.

But Cecilia wasn't asleep now.

She thought about the past six years, and how hard she'd fought not just to give Dante a good life, but to also make sure that her own didn't feel like an albatross around her neck. She'd chosen her life, and she'd made it good, with whatever pieces she'd had left after she'd had to leave the abbey.

And as much as she loved this man standing before her, as much as she'd always loved him and always would, she didn't see any reason why she should do any differently now.

She could, she knew. She could back off. She could say something placating, or try to smooth things over. She could continue this half-life she'd been living since she'd come to Rome with him. Wandering about aimlessly half the time, and then living for those moments when she woke up in his arms, and could pretend she was horrified to find herself there.

There were a thousand games that she could play, but she didn't want any of that.

She wanted him, not games.

She wanted their family.

She wanted everything that she'd told him she wanted, but she was greedy. She wanted him to want it, too. She'd grown up with a family of nuns, so she knew her way around a martyr. And she didn't want any of that, either.

She could accept anything. She could make anything work, and had.

But here, now, in this marriage that she could have resisted, but hadn't—all so she could have the pleasure of pretending he'd forced her into it—she was done accepting things. Working with whatever came her way. Making the best of it.

He tasted like everything she'd ever wanted, and that was what she wanted now. *Everything.* Cecilia had no intention of settling for anything less.

"No," she said.

Pascal stared at her in that frozen, arrogant way he had as if he assumed he must have misheard her. Because certainly no one could possibly dare cross him.

"No?" he echoed as if he didn't quite understand.

"I told you what I want." Her voice was distinct and steady. And she held his gaze. "And for once, Pascal, I'm not willing to settle for less. If it's too much for you, I understand. But I'm not running away from anything. If you can't handle this…"

And then her voice cracked, because she wasn't a machine. She was a woman, flesh and blood, and fighting for the man she loved the only way she knew how.

"If you don't know how to fight for us, I can't help you."

"Cecilia—"

"I'm not going anywhere," she told him. "Dante and I are staying put. But I won't stop you if you need to run away, Pascal. *Again.*"

Then, before she could change her mind and beg him all over again—and in a whole different way, possibly involving tears—Cecilia turned her back on him.

No matter how much it hurt.

And this time she was the one who walked away.

CHAPTER ELEVEN

PASCAL STOOD THERE for a long, long time after the door closed behind him.

After she'd left him the way he'd told her she should.

He stood there in that office that he'd been so proud of before. The office that represented who he was. All he had. All he was.

But instead of admiring the sharp, modern lines and their juxtaposition with ancient Rome right there outside his window, all he could see was Cecilia.

She was everything he'd ever wanted. Poise. Grace. Elegance.

And somehow, despite all that, she loved him.

She loved him.

How could she possibly love him?

Pascal could feel his heart kicking at him as if it was trying to beat him up from the inside out. He was hardly aware of it when he wheeled around, grabbing his heavy coat on the way out, and muttered something largely incomprehensible to Guglielmo.

He needed to get out. He needed to get away.

He threw himself into the streets, the way he always had.

Rome was his first love. The eternal city—and his eternal and only salvation. Rome was how he had learned who he was, what he could do. Rome had made him. There had been years Pascal had believed that only the battered old streets of this city knew him at all.

He walked and he walked, chasing the December day toward its brief afternoon. It was two days before Christmas and the weather was raw. Damp and cold. Still, it suited his mood. It matched the tumult within.

He navigated his way over slick stone and around knots of people. It seemed to him as he moved that he could feel the pulse of the city inside him, the whispers of three thousand years of so many lives. Hopes and dreams, loss and grief, all there beneath his feet.

It was as if the stones themselves seem to hum with all the life—and love—that had happened here. Too many times to count. Rome was stories that could never be told, lives tangled together and lost in time. Myths that anyone could recite and smaller, hidden tales no one would ever know. He could hear that humming everywhere. He could feel it shoot straight down his spine.

Then again, he thought as he found himself in a far-off *piazza* lit up with Christmas trees and a festive market, it could as easily be the carolers.

He stood there in a neighborhood he rarely visited, a part of the same grand mosaic of stories lost and found, lived and lost. And though it was not his custom to play the slightest attention to Christmas songs, or Christmas itself if he could avoid it, he found himself listening despite himself as they sang.

Songs of joy. Songs of peace.

Pascal had always preferred to believe they were lies...but the familiar songs didn't feel like a lie this gloomy evening. He did.

And maybe that was why, sometime later, he found himself in a neighborhood he usually preferred to avoid. And worse, standing outside the house he knew well though he had only ever seen it in pictures. There had been some dark years when he had set men on this house, to watch it. To report back. To give him a sense of what it was he fought.

He had sworn to himself that he would never come here himself. Never in person. Not after all those times his mother had come here when Pascal was a child, only to be turned away.

Over and over again as she wept that she was dirt.

Pascal had vowed that he would never allow his father the opportunity to do the same to him.

But it was a short, bitter sort of day, and the long night was already gathering. He looked through the lit-up windows at tidy, unremarkable rooms that indicated the owners were well-off—if not particularly flashy. Even here there were Christmas trees on display and festive decorations that looked as if they were part of a design feature, not the kind of family nostalgia he'd always assumed the people who lived here indulged in.

Mostly because he never would.

And then a man he'd seen in pictures—often in a split frame next to his own face but never in the flesh—walked into the main room and frowned as he looked around as if searching for a mislaid item.

Likely not his discarded son, Pascal thought bitterly. Never *that*.

He wasn't sure what he expected to see. A monster, perhaps. A worthy opponent, certainly. A focal point for everything he'd done and all the ways he'd gloried in rolling around in the dirt just to throw it here.

But all he saw in the bright windows was a shriveled old man. Alone.

And if the look on his face was any guide as he huffed around his little domain, an unhappy one to boot.

Once again Pascal felt as if the ground had been snatched out from beneath his feet, there where he stood in the narrow road as the darkness fell around him and the winter night grew colder.

For the first time—maybe ever, if he was honest—he had to ask himself why he had expended so much energy to build an entire life *at* this sad, tired, mean creature. The life he saw through the windows was so narrow. So small.

And exactly where you're headed, a voice inside him that sounded a lot like hers warned him.

Because all Pascal had done in all this time was make himself small, too.

And it was as if something vast opened up inside him then.

Cecilia.

She was endless. She had walked into his life and nothing had been the same. First, she had brought him to life. Then she had given him the tools to build an empire worthy of her, though it had cost her. And when he'd finally returned to her, haunted by her after all those years, she'd given him a son.

And today she'd told him she loved him, when no one else had ever tried.

She was more than beauty and she was deeper than truth. She was faith. She was hope.

But he'd let her walk away. And he'd come here instead, to watch an old man who had been given the whole of Pascal's lifetime to right a wrong, change his ways, offer a hand across a great divide…and hadn't.

Pascal felt twisted up with the things he didn't know today, but of one thing he was utterly sure. Whatever became of him, he did not want to end up like his father.

All he had to do was open up this death grip of his,

let the old man go, and choose. Not to be so small. Not to consign himself to the very same fate. Not to chase the same end the way he'd been doing all this time.

Because Pascal had a child, too.

And Dante was his chance to remake the world. Not to narrow it, choke it with hate, make it hurt and fight and plot revenge.

Dante was his chance to do the opposite. Instead of being the monster his father had been and ever would be, Pascal could be the father he had always wished he'd had.

There was only one way out of the dark and into the light.

All Pascal had to do was finally be man enough to take it.

He turned his back on the house. The man. The father so undeserving of that title. He began to walk, putting distance between him and the street where his mother had wailed to no avail. And as he moved, the dirt from that street that had been on him his whole life fell away, because it had never been his. It belonged where he'd found it.

And as he broke into a run, he knew without a shred of doubt that he would never return.

Pascal ran through the streets of his beloved city. The colors and the sounds, the stories and the songs, all began to blend. All the *piazzas* done up for Christmas, all the people in throngs and gathered in the cafés.

All of them out here in the December dark to bask, together, in the light they made to beat it back.

Hope. Faith.

Pascal finally understood.

He only hoped he wasn't too late.

When he made it to his home at last, he threw himself in through the door, staggering into his foyer. At first he hardly recognized the space, until he realized what she'd done. She'd brought it inside from the streets—the trees all lit up, the chaotic joy of it all. Evergreen trees made bright like a taunt—

Was this what she'd left him to remember her by?

Pascal was sure that she had gone already. That she had ordered the staff to decorate and had packed up Dante, then taken herself off, just as he'd told her to do. Because when he had been offered the choice to stay or leave, he'd left. Six years ago he'd simply left her.

Why shouldn't she do the same?

He shouted for his housekeeper, then shouted for his car—

"I let the housekeeper go tonight," came a voice from behind him. "She has her own family to decorate for."

Pascal turned, slowly. Because he was sure he was imagining it.

But she was there, walking toward him from the hall that led to Dante's suite.

"I just put Dante to bed," Cecilia said quietly

when she came to a stop before him, still dressed in the same clothes he'd seen on her—and off her—earlier. "You're shouting loud enough to wake the dead. One small boy will wake a whole lot more easily."

She was still here.

For a moment that was all that he could think about. It was all that mattered.

And as her words penetrated the mad, howling thing inside him, he realized that she clearly wasn't going anywhere—not tonight anyway—if she'd put Dante down to sleep.

He moved toward her, and he felt as if he had the weight of a thousand worlds clinging to each of his limbs as he moved. The world he'd grown up in. The world he'd made.

The world he'd left behind him tonight.

When he reached her, he put his hands on her shoulders as if he needed to assure himself that she was real.

Because he needed her to be real. He needed it more than air.

"Cecilia," he said, because her name was like a song and he'd been trying to get that particular tune out of his head for far too long.

Tonight he'd stopped trying.

And it was time to start singing it instead.

"Pascal," she whispered back, her wide violet eyes solemn.

And then, finally, while the storm raged inside

him and his bones ached with the effort, Pascal Furlani sang the only song that mattered.

He surrendered.

He sank down on his knees, took her hands in his and begged.

"Please don't leave me," he said, urgent and low. "I know I've given you no reason to stay, no reason to do anything but hate me. But Cecilia, I can't live without you. I've tried."

She shifted as if she would say something—

But he cut her off, because he couldn't stop now.

"I love you," he told her. "I built empires in your absence, but all I saw was your ghost. You have haunted me since the moment I woke up in pieces and saw you there, smiling. You taught me how to live. To love. To imagine that I could be the kind of man who could do either when I'd never thought I was much of anything but another man's dirt. I don't deserve you. I never will."

"Pascal—"

"Cecilia," he said, a song and a vow, and her—always her, "I need you to stay here. I need to become the man I imagined I was when I was smashed into a million pieces and you alone made me whole. I need to become that man so I can be the husband you deserve. The father Dante deserves. And I am very much afraid that only you can teach me how."

There were tears in the corners of her lovely eyes, and they chased each other down her cheeks as she sank down on her knees so she could be there with him in the sparkling light of so many Christmas trees.

"Pascal," she whispered. "Don't you understand? It's already done. I am your wife. That means you help me. And I help you. And we love each other, forever. That was what we promised."

"I know how to make money," he told her, the intensity in his voice inside him, too. "But what I want is to make you happy. To make our son happy. To make more babies, and make them happy, too."

"I want all of those things," she said. "And I want you happy, too. Pascal, you deserve to be happy."

"I don't deserve you," he managed to say. "I know that much."

Her hands smoothed over his face then. She traced his scars and she held his gaze, and the light he saw in her eyes humbled him. Exalted him.

Made him whole.

"You have hurt me more than I ever thought I could be hurt," she whispered fiercely. "But that could never have been possible if you hadn't also made me the happiest I've ever been. I have to think that that's the point. The hurt and the happiness. All of it wrapped up together. If we do it together, I think that's love."

And then he was kissing her, or she was kissing him. But they were together. And all of this was theirs, that fire, that need. All that brightness they made together, to banish the night, glowed between them.

Pascal began to imagine it always would.

"I promise you," he told her then, his voice as serious as his mouth was hot against hers. "I will never leave you again."

"I will never leave you, either," she replied in the same solemn way as if these were the vows that mattered, here on their knees in Rome with all the Christmas lights to guide them. "We will fight for each other, not against each other."

"You and me, my love," he agreed hoarsely. "That will make all the difference."

For each other, not against. Pascal felt that settle there inside him, deep into his bones.

Choose love, she'd implored him. *Just once.*

And finally, with everything he had and everything he hoped he would be, that was exactly what Pascal did.

He chose Cecilia.

Forever.

CHAPTER TWELVE

THREE YEARS LATER Pascal basked in the sweetness of another perfect Christmas Day.

Up in the mountains the brooding Dolomites stood tall, high above them. He was certain he could feel them there, even in the dark. They had impressed themselves upon him so completely that sometimes he thought he could feel them down in Rome.

He heard a soft sound and turned to see his beautiful wife coming into the room that was lit only by the fire on one side and a tall, gleaming Christmas tree on the other.

He had built her this cottage that was no cottage at all. He had set it outside the small village, up in the foothills, so they could gaze down upon the pretty valley together. The abbey, the church and all those beautiful fields that had been his only entertainment once.

The villagers muttered about rich men and their houses in the hills, but Pascal didn't care if they talked about him beneath their breath as long as they treated his wife as they should. And they did, because Cecilia was theirs no matter the rarefied air she breathed as Signora Furlani. And with every visit, they thawed toward her husband, too.

Pascal would have sworn he didn't care about such things. He wouldn't have once. But Cecilia cared deeply about the good opinion of the people here— and therefore, Pascal did, too.

There was no limit to the things he would do for her.

"Come," he said now, reaching out his hand. And his Cecilia could still smile at him the way she did now, making his world stop and shudder. "I have built us a fire."

She took his hand and let him draw her close, then lead her over toward the fire.

"Dante told me he was not sleepy at all and would stay up all night, to spite me if necessary," Cecilia confided with a laugh. "But he was out before I turned off the light."

Dante was eight now, filled with his father's stubborn purpose. Pascal anticipated that he would always be the way he was now, prepared to butt heads at the slightest provocation—and also the quickest to apologize and the first to declare his affection. Even thinking of the boy made Pascal smile.

"And Giulia?" Pascal asked, his smile widening

as he thought of their headstrong and deeply beloved two-year-old daughter.

"Dead to the world," Cecilia said happily.

Pascal pulled her into his arms, then down onto the rug before the fire. They stretched out together as the flames leaped and danced in the grate. And Cecilia sighed at the way they fit, the way she always did.

Because years might have passed, but the spark between them never took more than the simplest touch to build up into the flames that could still burn them both to ash. And sometimes it took only a look.

Pascal had learned how to work less, but Cecilia worked more. That first year, unable to remain idle, or any kind of ornament, she had started her own charity for orphans and foundlings all over the world.

Sometimes that meant Pascal got to be the trophy on her arm, which he found he greatly enjoyed.

More than that, he found it nothing but entertaining to watch her innate grace up against dedicated sharks like his board members. Or against the inevitable slings and arrows of the mercurial press, who loved them one day then hated them the next.

Cecilia handled them all the same. With that quiet steel of hers that had brought him to his knees once. And always would.

She had made him far better than he deserved to be. And he worked every day to make sure she never regretted her choices.

Last night at midnight mass in the church down

on the valet floor, Mother Superior had smiled at him the way she did these days. Fondly. She clasped his hands in her old, gnarled grip, and she'd called him *child*.

Pascal would die before he admitted how much he liked that.

"Fear is always a liar. Love is always the truth," she'd said, that same ring of steel in her kind voice that she'd bequeathed to his wife. "I cannot tell you how it delights me to watch you live that."

"Every day," he'd said, like a new vow. "And always."

Because every day he remembered all those things he'd thought he wanted when he'd stood on the edge of the field that he could see from his windows here on a clear day. When he'd looked at the little boy who didn't know him, running heedless on the frozen grass, and wanted more than he'd ever been given himself.

He remembered the notion he'd had that he was looking at something huge, and how desperately he'd hoped he could find a way to cram it all inside him. To make it work.

God, how he'd wanted it to fit.

Because he hadn't understood then. The things he'd taken for tears were oceans, too massive to be crammed inside him or any one person. There was a vastness that couldn't fit anywhere, and that was the point.

Love grows and grows and grows, he thought as Cecilia lay beside him. It got better all the time. Especially when she tipped her face to his and kissed him.

She smiled against his mouth as he ran his hands along her sides, then over her sweet belly where she'd carried his babies.

And he knew she was keeping another secret. That she would tell him when she was sure, that it was early days yet. But he knew.

He estimated it would be about another seven months before they welcomed another member of the family. But Pascal was happy to take his time unwrapping her secrets, one after the next, until they were like the mountains he could feel out there in the dark. Standing sentry against the passage of time.

Love and hope, ageless and eternal.

Just as they would be to each other. Come what may.

"I love you," Cecilia whispered as she moved against him.

"I love you," he replied.

And it would grow and grow and grow, for the rest of their lives, and on into their children—bright as the light that turned back the night, gleaming on into always, just like Christmas.

* * * * *

If you enjoyed
Unwrapping the Innocent's Secret
by Caitlin Crews
you're sure to enjoy these other
Secret Heirs of Billionaires stories!

Demanding His Hidden Heir
by Jackie Ashenden

The Maid's Spanish Secret
by Dani Collins

Sheikh's Royal Baby Revelation
by Annie West

Cinderella's Scandalous Secret
by Melanie Milburne

Available now

Available November 19, 2019

#3769 THE GREEK'S SURPRISE CHRISTMAS BRIDE
Conveniently Wed!
by Lynne Graham

Letty can't let her family fall into financial ruin. A convenient Christmas wedding with Leo is the ideal solution! Until their paper-only arrangement is scorched...by the heat of their unanticipated attraction!

#3770 THE QUEEN'S BABY SCANDAL
One Night With Consequences
by Maisey Yates

Mauro is stunned to discover the beautiful innocent who left his bed at midnight three months ago is a queen...and she's pregnant! He's never wanted a family, but nothing will stop this billionaire from demanding his heir.

#3771 PROOF OF THEIR ONE-NIGHT PASSION
Secret Heirs of Billionaires
by Louise Fuller

Ragnar's chaotic childhood inspired his billion-dollar dating app. He must keep romantic attachments simple. But when Lottie reveals their heart-stopping encounter had consequences, there's no question that Ragnar *will* claim his baby...

#3772 SECRET PRINCE'S CHRISTMAS SEDUCTION
by Carol Marinelli

Prince Rafe is floored by his unexpected connection to chambermaid Antonietta. All he can offer is a temporary seduction. But unwrapping the precious gift of her virginity changes *everything*. Now Rafe must choose—his crown, or Antonietta...

HPCNMRA1119

#3773 A DEAL TO CARRY THE ITALIAN'S HEIR
The Scandalous Brunetti Brothers
by Tara Pammi
With her chances of finally having a family in jeopardy, Neha's taking drastic action! Approaching Leonardo with her outrageous request to father her child by IVF is step one. Step two? Ignoring her deep desire for him!

#3774 CHRISTMAS CONTRACT FOR HIS CINDERELLA
by Jane Porter
Duty has always dictated Marcu's actions, making free-spirited Monet, with her infamous family history, strictly forbidden. But when their long-simmering passion burns intensely enough to melt the snow, will Marcu claim his Christmas Cinderella...?

#3775 SNOWBOUND WITH HIS FORBIDDEN INNOCENT
by Susan Stephens
Snowed-in with Stacey, his best friend's untouched—and very off-limits!—sister, Lucas discovers temptation like no other. And as their mutual attraction grows hotter, Lucas has never been so close to breaking the rules...

#3776 MAID FOR THE UNTAMED BILLIONAIRE
Housekeeper Brides for Billionaires
by Miranda Lee
Being suddenly swept into Jake's world—and his arms!—is an eye-opening experience for shy maid Abby. But when Jake's number one rule is *no long-term relationships*, how can Abby possibly tame the wild billionaire?

Get 4 FREE REWARDS!

We'll send you 2 FREE Books plus 2 FREE Mystery Gifts.

HARLEQUIN
Presents.

USA TODAY BESTSELLING AUTHOR
Annie West
Sheikh's Royal Baby Revelation

HARLEQUIN
Presents.

NEW YORK TIMES BESTSELLING AUTHOR
Maisey Yates
His Forbidden Pregnant Princess

Harlequin Presents® books feature a sensational and sophisticated world of international romance where sinfully tempting heroes ignite passion.

FREE Value Over **$20**

YES! Please send me 2 FREE Harlequin Presents® novels and my 2 FREE gifts (gifts are worth about $10 retail). After receiving them, if I don't wish to receive any more books, I can return the shipping statement marked "cancel." If I don't cancel, I will receive 6 brand-new novels every month and be billed just $4.55 each for the regular-print edition or $5.80 each for the larger-print edition in the U.S., or $5.49 each for the regular-print edition or $5.99 each for the larger-print edition in Canada. That's a savings of at least 11% off the cover price! It's quite a bargain! Shipping and handling is just 50¢ per book in the U.S. and $1.25 per book in Canada.* I understand that accepting the 2 free books and gifts places me under no obligation to buy anything. I can always return a shipment and cancel at any time. The free books and gifts are mine to keep no matter what I decide.

Choose one: ☐ **Harlequin Presents®**
Regular-Print
(106/306 HDN GNWY)

☐ **Harlequin Presents®**
Larger-Print
(176/376 HDN GNWY)

Name (please print)

Address   Apt. #

City   State/Province   Zip/Postal Code

Mail to the Reader Service:
IN U.S.A.: P.O. Box 1341, Buffalo, NY 14240-8531
IN CANADA: P.O. Box 603, Fort Erie, Ontario L2A 5X3

Want to try 2 free books from another series? Call 1-800-873-8635 or visit www.ReaderService.com.

Lottie Dawson is stunned to see her daughter's father on television. She'd lost hope of finding the irresistible stranger after their incredible night of passion. Having never known her own father, Lottie wants things to be different for her child, even if that means facing Ragnar Stone again!

Read on for a sneak preview of
Louise Fuller's next story for Harlequin Presents
Proof of Their One-Night Passion

The coffee shop was still busy enough that they had to queue for their drinks, but they managed to find a table.

"Thank you." He gestured toward his espresso.

His wallet had been in his hand, but she had sidestepped neatly in front of him, her soft brown eyes defying him to argue with her. Now, though, those same brown eyes were busily avoiding his, and for the first time since she'd called out his name, he wondered why she had tracked him down.

He drank his coffee, relishing the heat and the way the caffeine started to block the tension in his back.

"So, I'm all yours," he said quietly.

She stiffened. "Hardly."

He sighed. "Is that what this is about? Me giving you the wrong name."

Her eyes narrowed. "No, of course not. I'm not—" She stopped, frowning. "Actually, I wasn't just passing, and I'm not here for myself." She took a breath. "I'm here for Sóley."

Her face softened into a smile and he felt a sudden urge to reach out and caress the curve of her lip, to trigger such a smile for himself.

"It's a pretty name."

She nodded, her smile freezing.

It was a pretty name—one he'd always liked. One you didn't hear much outside of Iceland. Only what had it got to do with him?

Watching her fingers tremble against her cup, he felt his ribs tighten. "Who's Sóley?"

She was quiet for less than a minute, only it felt much longer—long enough for his brain to click through all the possible answers to the impossible one. The one he already knew.

He watched her posture change from defensive to resolute.

"She's your daughter. Our daughter."

He stared at her in silence, but a cacophony of questions was ricocheting inside his head.

Not the how or the when or the where, but the why. Why had he not been more careful? Why had he allowed the heat of their encounter to blot out his normally ice-cold logic?

But the answers to those questions would have to wait.

"Okay..."

Shifting in her seat, she frowned. "'Okay'?" she repeated. "Do you understand what I just said?"

"Yes." He nodded. "You're saying I got you pregnant."

"You don't seem surprised," she said slowly.

He shrugged. "These things happen."

To his siblings and half siblings, even to his mother. But not to him. Never to him.

Until now.

"And you believe me?" She seemed confused, disappointed?

Tilting his head, he held her gaze. "Honest answer?"

He was going to ask her what she would gain by lying. But before he could open his mouth, her lip curled.

"On past performance, I'm not sure I can expect that. I mean, you lied about your name. And the hotel you were staying at. And you lied about wanting to spend the day with me."

"I didn't plan on lying to you," he said quietly.

Her mouth thinned. "No, I'm sure it comes very naturally to you."

"You're twisting my words."

She shook her head. "You mean like saying Steinn instead of Stone?"

Pressing his spine into the wall behind him, he felt a tick of anger begin to pulse beneath his skin.

"Okay, I was wrong to lie to you—but if you care about the truth so much, then why have you waited so long to tell me that I have a daughter? I mean, she must be what...?" He did a quick mental calculation. "Ten, eleven months?"

Don't miss
Proof of Their One-Night Passion
available December 2019 wherever
Harlequin Presents® books and ebooks are sold.

www.Harlequin.com